NAKED CAME THE
POST-POSTMODERNIST

NAKED CAME THE POST-POSTMODERNIST

A Mystery by

SARAH LAWRENCE COLLEGE
WRITING CLASS WRIT-3303-R

TAUGHT BY
MELVIN JULES BUKIET

Arcade Publishing • New York

First Edition

Arcade Publishing books may be purchased in bulk at special discounts for sales promotion, corporate gifts, fund-raising, or educational purposes. Special editions can also be created to specifications. For details, contact the Special Sales Department, Arcade Publishing, 307 West 36th Street, 11th Floor, New York, NY 10018 or arcade@skyhorsepublishing.com.

Arcade Publishing® is a registered trademark of Skyhorse Publishing, Inc.®, a Delaware corporation.

Visit our website at www.arcadepub.com.

10 9 8 7 6 5 4 3 2 1

Library of Congress Cataloging-in-Publication Data

Naked Came the Post-Postmodernist / Sarah Lawrence College, Writing Class WRIT-3303-R ; taught by Melvin Jules Bukiet. —First edition.
    pages cm
"By the students of class WRIT-3303-R, 2012-2013 academic year, Sarah Lawrence College"
ISBN 978-1-61145-909-8 (alk. paper)
1. College teachers—Crimes against—Fiction. 2. Mystery fiction. I. Bukiet, Melvin Jules.
PS3600.A1N355 2013
813'.6-dc23   2013030536

Printed in the United States of America

Contents

Editorial Assistant: Sasha Pezenik

NAKED CAME THE
POST-POSTMODERNIST

1.

Detective Harsley knelt before the washing machine as if inspecting a victim's entrails. Slimy blue detergent covered his work shirts.

"Goddamn," he swore under his breath as he crawled behind it, deeper into the basement. His off-white boxers hung loosely on his frame, and his bare knees scuffed painfully against the grainy cement floor. Something was wrong with the hot water tube. It was a problem that had occurred multiple times over the last year, yet he had never been able to fix it himself. Fifteen minutes of a plumber's hour cost two days of a cop's wages.

As he examined a knot of wires in the back, he heard a faint ringing from upstairs. He paused, surprised at how strange the noise sounded. Then again, he had rarely used the house phone or given the number out since his ex-wife had insisted on buying matching cell phones. That was the year they moved to Waldham and still liked each other enough to be thrilled at the idea of doing it in all of the rooms.

"Bitch," he muttered under his breath as he thought of her. Knees cracking, he stood and trudged to the threadbare maroon-carpeted stairs, casting one last glance at the soggy, multi-armed tangle of shirts.

Harsley doubted Lisa still had that phone. Ronnie the insurance man would have bought her a new, sleeker model. Harsley imagined the two of them in their three-story house on the other side of town. Lisa was giving Robbie head in front of the TV so he could see last night's scores while she attended to him. Or some shit like that.

He opened the door that led from the basement stairs into the kitchen and stepped onto the well-polished wooden floor. The boards were so smooth that his bare feet felt rough against them, his heels bulbous and hard. He stood in front of the phone, staring at the blackened arcs and indents on the buttons Lisa had touched most frequently before she left. The numbers 4 and 7 were especially grimy. Humans are filthy, he thought. That's why getting away with killing them is so difficult. They leave their filth everywhere. Dirty bodies. Dirty thoughts.

He reached out and answered the phone. "Yes?"

"Detective Harsley?"

"Who's this?"

He glanced at his reflection in the sliding glass door. Slight curves of muscles were visible beneath his skin, but they appeared to be buried deeper every day. He had always fancied the notion that his body was like a piece of marble that had never been completely chiseled into its ultimate shape. He remembered reading about ancient sculptors who could see what was meant to be created out of a piece of stone even when it was just a big square block. This was how he had always regarded his body—the slight double chin and the extra curl of fat at the base of his stomach were merely extraneous pieces that hadn't yet been chipped away. Since Lisa had left he told himself he didn't care, but he did.

"Sir? You there? It's Carl." The voice took form.

"Oh. Carl." Harsley stopped looking at his reflection and observed what lay beyond; the backyard was gummy with springtime and humidity. "Why didn't you call my cell?" he asked.

"I did," Carl answered.

"Oh," Harsley said. He decided he would buy a barbecue. That would fit nicely in the corner of the yard. He would invite the neighbors over, and maybe the woman with the hair that always smelled like pineapple and the charmingly tight skirts would stay later and they'd have sex on the living room floor. Or on the icebox, or the couch. Wherever she preferred.

"There's been a murder at that school in Hurst Green." Carl's voice sounded strangely robotic to Harsley. He wasn't sure why.

"Underhill College?" he asked. His brain switched directions instantly. This was why he was good at his job. An investigative checklist began scrolling behind his eyelids: blood spatter, knives, guns, access cards, security guards, parking lots.

"Your guess is as good as mine." Carl half-chuckled. "I don't think I've ever been to Hurst Green."

"Rich like you couldn't imagine," Harsley muttered. "I suppose their cops asked for some help? I'm guessing they don't have many murders over there."

"Said they'd appreciate our outside position. Apparently their detective is on vacation."

Harsley could tell Carl was grinning, as if working for the force in Waldham let him into the cool kids group.

"Well?" Harsley asked.

Carl coughed. "Right. Some professor at the school found dead in his office. Could be a natural death, but judging by the frothing around the mouth forensics thinks it's most likely a poisoning. We won't know until we get him back to the morgue."

"Who called it in?"

Harsley heard Carl ruffling through paper.

"Grace. Grace Montoya. A student of his," he said.

"And the vic?"

"A math professor. She said his name was Davenport."

Harsley watched a plane inch across the gray New England sky. "You think they were fucking?" he asked, almost with a sigh.

"Huh?"

"First name."

"Oh." Carl paused. "I don't know."

Harsley twirled a pen in his stubby fingers. He seldom took notes, but he liked to have something in hand to play with. Carl was efficient and reliable in his work but lacked the intuition necessary to be a good detective. Of course, there would be the possibility of a sexual relationship, Harsley thought. That was always a good motive for a murder.

"You said he was a math professor?" Harsley asked, returning his focus to the matter at hand.

"Yeah," Carl replied.

Harsley chuckled. "Didn't know they taught math at liberal arts schools."

"Huh?"

"Never mind."

There was a pause. "Uniforms have taped off the area," Carl said hesitantly. "They'll start canvassing soon. Meet you over there?"

Carl sounded more human now. Harsley wasn't sure what had changed. "Sure," he agreed. "Text me the address."

After he hung up, Harsley stood motionless in the kitchen in his boxers. He was sure he had dreamt this scene before but couldn't remember when or the exact details.

The coffee pot hissed and gurgled to a finish. He went to the counter and poured a cup and then paused and took down a thermos. He had one sip of the coffee and poured the rest into the thermos and set the cup in the sink. Stained and barely used, it seemed stripped of purpose and somehow lonely. Shut up, Harsley thought. Just 'cause you're lonely doesn't mean the damn cup is. Besides, forensics will be at the site, which means Kate, too. Maybe she'll be wearing that shirt I like, the one that outlines her tits so perfectly. He went into his room to change and found the only button-up he owned that wasn't smeared with blue gunk. Ten minutes later he got into his 1992

Honda with manual locks and depressed the cigarette lighter. He waited until the electric ring heated and then lit a Camel.

During the drive Harsley blasted the AC. The radio was off. He was sure Carl was already trying to piece things together, even before he saw the body. That was a common mistake, Harsley felt. Most men wanted to be one step ahead. Best to wait and then let his instincts guide him. His palms were sweaty, but the response wasn't unusual. He wiped them, one and then the other, on the thigh of his pants. The car was filled with cold air and smoke. He cracked the window.

When Harsley took the exit from 95 onto Mapleton Avenue, he noted the sudden difference in atmosphere. He had always loved this about cities and their respective suburbs—one street on the brink of gentrification, the next a wasteland. Streets where the sidewalk could seem cleaner or richer than the block before, even though it had been paved at the same time with the same cement. One stretch sparkled, the next had so many black gum spots it looked like a flattened Dalmatian.

Mapleton was a road he wouldn't have been surprised to see in a movie set in the countryside, perhaps in England. The clouds in Waldham that morning had never released any rain, but the cement in Hurst Green looked damp. Perhaps the weather is different here, Harsley thought. Or maybe the town pays illegal immigrants to hose the streets every morning for that fresh, glistening look.

Small roads branched off to the right, winding by large Georgian or Greek Revival–style homes. The driveways were cobbled. The kind of pavement that is particularly noisy,

Harsley noted. Hurst Green was the type of place where every-thing had been built to be majestic rather than practical. That made murder harder to get away with. A poisoning made sense.

Harsley turned a corner and saw a sign pointing toward the administration building for Underhill College. Students in torn sweaters and large leather boots meandered up a sloping hill to his right. Their ragged appearance may have seemed odd compared to the wealth of the surroundings, but Harsley could tell their presentation was calculated: messi-ness made possible by privilege—you pay more for the holes. He shook his head, tapping the ash of his cigarette onto the passenger seat.

The students appeared to be going about their daily routines. Harsley wondered if they'd been told about the misbehavior in their midst. He glanced at them as he drove by. A boy with a large stud in his nose walked alongside a girl with curious hair. When the boy burst into laughter, Harsley thought there was something animalistic about his smile. He couldn't tell if the girl beside the young rhino looked happy or not.

He checked his phone and took a right and then a left on Compton Street. There were more students and a series of school buildings rising up on the crest of a hill to his left like ramparts. "Shit," he muttered. "A place this rich, what do they have to kill about?"

A group of uniforms were clustered at the bottom of the hill, and he parked his car on the side of the narrow road. He stepped out, cigarette smoke billowing around him, and spotted Carl moving toward him.

"There's a parking lot around the corner," Carl said, looking at Harsley's car, which took up a third of the road. Harsley shrugged.

"Right," Carl continued as if he wanted to take Harsley's actions with complete nonchalance. What was he trying to prove? Harsley wondered. He ran his eyes briefly over Carl. Clean tie, tightly knotted. Two pens in the breast pocket. Hair ruffled but clearly cut recently. Moderately smart man who knew just how hard to work and just how hard to appear to be working. The kind of guy who'd always been happy, even as a teenager. Good looking. He had probably slept at a woman's house the night before, and left early enough for a run and a protein shake. Before coming here.

"The body's this way," Carl said, motioning.

"Lead on," Harsley said, gesturing with his wrist, as if he were bowing.

Carl gave him a strange look. Harsley flicked the stub of his cigarette onto the ground, exhaling long and loud.

A young man immediately picked up the cigarette and put it in his pocket and walked away.

Harsley shoved past Carl and strode toward a large Gothic building on the far side of the courtyard. Carl followed.

"It's there," Carl said, pointing at a doorway off the west wing of the building. Harsley opened the door and let Carl walk through first. Offices lined a hallway that stretched to the left and right. On the doors were little plaques with professors' names in black lettering. There was yellow tape across the office farthest on the left. Harsley glanced at the doorknob on their way in. It was old and made of brass. There were probably over a thousand fingerprints on it. Good luck forensics, he thought.

The body, average in size and shape, was in good condition. It was face down, the head resting on the left side, the right arm raised, its index finger outstretched from an otherwise clenched palm.

"Eric, right?" Harsley asked, walking around the body.

"His name? Yeah. Eric Davenport." Carl flipped through his notes. "He'd been teaching here for about twelve years."

"Forty-seven?" Harsley muttered.

"Huh?"

"About forty-seven years old?"

"Oh. Errr . . ." Carl went to the cluttered desk and picked up a wallet with a handkerchief. He pulled out an ID. "Yeah," he said with an awkward laugh. "In April."

Harsley snorted and wedged his foot underneath the body to roll it over.

"Sir, you should let forensics do that," Carl said.

Harsley ignored him and squatted. There were no signs of a struggle. "Carl," he said, "what kind of person would poison you?"

Carl coughed and laughed awkwardly. "Sir?"

"I mean, the kind of person who can get away with poisoning you is the kind of person you wouldn't expect it from."

"So Eric must have known his killer."

Harsley shrugged. "Most likely. Also, unless you happen to be carrying some curare in your vest pocket when the mood hits, poison implies premeditation." Harsley glanced at his watch. "What did the student say when she called it in?"

Carl looked at his notes. "She said she came in for her weekly conference—apparently that's what it's called here, where the students meet with their professors one-on-one—and found him like this."

"And she thought it was a natural death?"

"I'm not sure. She told the 911 operator that her professor was dead. But when the cops got here and asked her what happened she said he'd been murdered."

Harsley stared at the body for a moment. "So perhaps she knew what the frothing at the corner of the mouth meant."

"Maybe."

Harsley stood, rubbing his hands together.

"Sir, how could you tell his age?" Carl was still standing at his side.

Harsley sighed, examining the room. It was small and orderly, two chairs placed close together beside the window. "The shoulders," he said, still looking around. "The way they fill the jacket. Broad, but starting to sag; Hair at the back of the neck turning gray while the rest is pure black."

"What does that mean?"

Harsley glanced at Carl. Stupid, he thought. Stupid and lucky. The best things to be. "Eric still had an ego," he said with a sigh. "He wasn't ready to submit to being the 'old professor' yet."

"But why forty-seven? That could happen at lots of ages."

"He was on the edge." Harsley shrugged. "Partially fact, partially a guess. Instincts." He rummaged through his pocket and found an empty pack of cigarettes and crumpled it. "Got a smoke?"

Carl reached into his jacket and pulled out two cigarettes, handing one to Harsley.

"The murderer wasn't in a hurry. Wasn't worried at all," Carl muttered through the cigarette as he lit it. A puff of smoke curled up around his gray eyes and sandy hair.

Harsley could tell that Carl was the kind of guy who got laid all the time. He reached out to accept the lighter, imagining for a moment the kind of woman Carl would go home with.

"No forced entry, no surfaces rubbed down," Carl continued. "Whoever it was didn't feel the need to cover their tracks."

Carl got laid so often he didn't even need to think about it while he was working, Harsley decided. Lucky bastard. He exhaled.

Fucking low-tar.

"So it had to be someone he knew, someone who had been in his office before. They would have known there are all sorts of fingerprints here."

Harsley nodded. "Good," he said. He walked around the room once more, pausing at the window. It overlooked the small courtyard he had walked through. The courtyard had wooden tables and trees whose branches were thick with blossoms. From the outside no one was able to look into the office. Spring was a good season to kill in Hurst Green.

"Where's the girl?" he asked.

"Outside. Want to talk to her?"

Harsley nodded. Carl led the way. The hall was long and lit with dim fluorescence. The fixtures must be old, Harsley thought. There was an elevator next to a bulletin board crammed with overlapping announcements for mathematics programs abroad. One read, "Fibonacci in Fiorenza."

"Are these the only ways out?"

Carl glanced over his shoulder at the elevator. "That and the door we came through."

"Well, obviously."

Carl didn't reply for a moment. "It's a big building," he said eventually. "The main cafeteria is upstairs, as well as lots of administrative offices above that."

On their way out they ran into the ME that Harsley had expected. Kate Steelford was wearing a large coat, so the detective couldn't tell what shirt was beneath it. Her hair wasn't quite straight, but wasn't greasy either. She had showered yesterday but not this morning. Was there no time or had she been somewhere else?

She nodded at Harsley in acknowledgment, and as she walked between them he caught a small smile passing between her and Carl.

Carl held the door open for Harsley. "After you," he said.

"No, that's all right," Harsley replied. Stop being a child, he thought.

Carl stood awkwardly for a moment and then stepped around the door. The air was already more humid.

"How was she?" Harsley asked, walking out after him.

"What?" Carl replied, his neck reddening.

Harsley nodded back toward Kate.

Carl ignored him. "The girl's over there," he said, pointing to a student with hoop earrings and a bag large enough to hold an unabridged *Britannica* and a laptop. She was wearing a gray sweater with a few holes in the shoulders. Harsley patted Carl on the back and walked over to her. When he got there, the officer who had been talking to her nodded and left.

The girl was pretty in her own way. Harsley supposed if she were more comfortable in her skin she would have been more attractive. But it was clear she was a typical American girl who had been trying to lose five pounds ever since the beginning of high school. A girl who sometimes was happy and sometimes was sad and didn't understand why men desired her but readily accepted their half-hearted pursuit.

"Detective Harsley," Harsley said, reaching out to shake her hand.

She took it, smiling weakly. "Grace."

Her fingers were smaller than he had expected, more delicate.

"How are you doing today, Grace?"

She shook her head, a motion so small it seemed like an echo. Her eyebrows were raised. They were darker than her hair. "Um," she said. "I'm all right, I guess."

"A little shocked, no doubt?"

She raised her eyes to his. "Wouldn't you be?"

He felt a rush of blood but kept his eyes locked on hers. "Couldn't say," he said. "I've never found a dead body."

"But you find the killer."

"Sometimes."

Grace gazed across the courtyard at some indistinct point. "It's just, like . . ." She trailed off. "I can't stop imagining all the other ways Eric could have died."

Harsley dropped his cigarette on the ground and stubbed it out with his toe. Fascinating, he thought. "What do you mean?" he asked.

"Like, there are millions of other ways it could have gone. He could have grown old and gotten Alzheimer's or he could have been hit by a car last month or like . . . anything." Grace sighed. "I don't get it."

"Is this how you kids are taught to think?" Harsley asked.

Grace looked back up at him and returned his smile. She was prettier that way, Harsley thought.

"He was a math teacher. He didn't teach us to think. Or not like the other kinds of classes here."

"Was this your first class with him?"

Grace shook her head. "No, I've taken him for two years now."

"So you'd say you were close?"

Grace shifted inside her sweater. "All the students here are close with their professors."

"All right."

They were silent for a moment. Grace didn't seem uncomfortable. "Did you notice anything unusual about the room when you first went in?" Harsley asked.

"I mean," Grace replied, "besides the obvious?"

Harsley smiled. There was something more to her than he had initially guessed. She was quick, and somehow cruel, even in her shock. He nodded.

"He was always running over. The boy who had conference before me was in there for an extra ten minutes every week." Grace sighed. "But that's not unusual here."

"But the boy wasn't there today, was he?"

"No. At first I thought they were caught up in conversation again. But when I knocked nobody answered. So I waited a few minutes and then I just went in."

Harsley watched her.

She leaned back on the rock. "But somebody missing a conference isn't weird, either," she said.

Harsley wondered what *was* considered weird in this place. He observed her for a moment longer. "Thank you for your time, Miss Montoya," he said eventually. He waited, hoping she would tell him to call her Grace, but she didn't. He walked away. Carl was standing by the gate. He had lit another cigarette.

Harsley coughed lightly. "Who is Davenport's next of kin?" he asked.

Carl shrugged. "I'm not sure, sir. We haven't received his file yet. Why?"

"No ring," Harsley said. He squinted out the gate toward the road that came to a T twenty feet beyond them, as though he were already bored by their conversation.

"Maybe he wasn't married," Carl offered.

Harsley looked at Carl deploringly. "His suit jacket was ironed. There was a box of cherry blossom green tea on the windowsill."

"No picture of the wife," Carl countered.

"Exactly," Harsley said with a smug smile.

"What?" Carl replied exasperatedly.

"Put it together."

"You think that was intentional? That the killer took the photo?"

Harsley ran his hands across his face. "Everything's intentional. Especially in crime, and most of all in murder."

Carl watched him thoughtfully. "Is that why you're a detective?"

Harsley concealed a smile. Carl was trying to figure him out. That meant he had something Carl didn't. Harsley thought about Grace's cruel smile. "Because things add up?" Harsley clarified.

"Yeah," Carl replied.

"Maybe." Harsley grinned absent-mindedly. "Though Eric would have probably said the same about his life. What do you make of that?"

Carl glanced toward Kate, who was making her way across the courtyard. Harsley watched him.

"Not a lot," Carl said. "It's not so strange for men to want the same thing."

Harsley followed Carl's gaze. "Exactly."

REBECCA SHEPARD

2.

Sometimes things can't be explained. All the knowledge compiled throughout human existence is only a small island in a churning, infinite sea. And when the angry squall sends its black waves and threatens to engulf the island, the lonely inhabitants can do one of two things. They can bury their heads in the sand and stop their ears with all they previously held to be true. Or they can stand on the shore and stare down the tempest, even if it means their death.

Kate Steelford belonged to the latter group.

Kate's cell phone rang at two in the morning. When Kate turned on the light, Carl mumbled grumpily and rolled over. The white sheet slid down his hip, and the light from Kate's bedside table cast a finger of shadow along his naked spine. He had come to her apartment after work and cooked her dinner: rosemary chicken and couscous. Kate played some George Shearing and laughed when he put on one of her aprons and danced, snapping her tongs like castanets. They drank a lot of wine and played a lot of music to make up for the lack of conversation. They had been sleeping together for a couple of weeks, and despite the romantic gestures Kate knew the relationship would go no further. And when it ended he might be upset, but he was attractive enough that he would soon find another woman's bed and forget all about her. But for now he was a kind, capering distraction that lent Kate body heat and a mental vacancy that offered a sort of peace. Being with him was like floating on her back in an endless gray ocean, with no thoughts or sounds or ripples to disturb her. Plus he was a damn good cook.

But now her cell phone was vibrating like a buzz saw, and she had a sharp pain in her head from the wine. The name the cell phone showed was Harsley. She answered, "What?"

Harsley was irritated. His voice was gravelly and strained. "There's no need for the attitude, Steelford."

Kate sighed and rubbed her eyes. "It's two in the morning, Harsley. What do you want that can't wait another five hours?"

"Listen, princess, I'm not calling just to shoot the shit."

"Just tell me what you want or I'm hanging up."

She heard him take a deep breath, controlling his urge to snap at her, and he said, "I need access to the body of that math teacher from Underhill. And I want you to do an autopsy."

"What? Harsley, the body is scheduled for an autopsy tomorrow. Can't you just—"

Harsley let out a frustrated cough and said, "No, I need it done now. Meet me at County Medical in half an hour. Don't bring Carl."

Kate's brow furrowed. She'd made Carl promise not to say anything about their liaisons, especially to Harsley. "Did he say—?"

"Forget about it. Just get your ass to the morgue." He hung up. Kate sighed and rubbed her temples, trying to get the pain to subside. The last thing she wanted to do right now was to cut open some stiff and dig around while that dirty old bastard stared down her blouse. But if she ignored him and went back to sleep, he would keep calling, or worse, drive to her apartment. Then she would have to shoot him.

Kate smiled at her private joke as she slid quietly out of bed, careful not to wake Carl. She hoped he would be gone whenever she got back so she could shower and eat breakfast alone. She dressed by the table light. She was fit, and her curves were bathed in shadow as she pulled her clothes on. If she had spent time in the presence of people with aesthetic sensibilities, she might have been recognized for her classic, natural beauty. But her lot was the gruff dispensers of justice who dealt in the bloody consequences of human interactions. It's hard to truly appreciate surface beauty once you've seen what spills out when sharp edges are applied.

She paused, deciding between a blouse or a turtleneck. She thought about Harsley's bloodshot eyes and his leering smirk. Fuck him, she thought, if he needs me this goddamn early, he'll have to do without his private peep show.

*

When Kate finally arrived at the county morgue after dealing with the thick-headed midnight watchman, her mood had not improved. She signed the forms for an autopsy, knowing that

her boss would chew her out in the morning. But that was preferable to Harsley's wrath. He'd been waiting for her in the lobby
with a half-smoked cigarette behind his ear. He was wearing an
overcoat and sporting a five o'clock shadow, both gray. He was a
dark presence over the sleek white tiles of the waiting room. He
didn't say a word, only followed her to the morgue in a brooding
silence. But Kate sensed that his mood wasn't her fault. She had
been around him enough times and heard Carl talk about him
enough to know when he was being grumpy or thinking hard.
Perv though he was, he was also a damn good detective.

"So," Kate said, "you going to tell me what this is all about?"

Harsley removed the half-smoked cigarette from behind
his ear and rolled it between his thumb and forefinger. "I just
need the autopsy. Look for anything out of the ordinary."

"You can't smoke in the morgue, genius," Kate said, walking ahead.

"I know. I'm not a fucking idiot." But he continued to roll
the half cigarette between his fingers.

"And this couldn't wait till day?"

"No."

"Damnit, Harsley, there's something you're not telling me.
And *you* called *me* at two in the morning, remember?"

"Tough titties."

They stopped outside the locker room, and Kate swiped
her ID card in the scrubs machine. She pulled the folded green
linen out of the slot and said, "I need to change. Wait here."

Harsley grinned and asked, "You want some help?"

"Fuck you."

*

They slid open the metal drawer and moved Eric Davenport's body to a metal examining table, where it now lay under the bright lamp. He was no longer exhibiting rigor, and in a day or two outside of cold storage he would start to bloat and smell. His fingernails and hair had grown slightly since his death, giving him a rough, wild look, like he might spring up and grasp your collar, demanding to know why he had died.

Kate pulled on the rubber gloves, thinking, No wonder people believe in vampires.

Harsley scanned the body dispassionately. Kate saw his eyes linger on the penis for a brief second before moving away. Something about the genitalia of dead people was particularly morbid, the signifier of sex and procreation lying wasted, soon to be worm food. Celebrities and millionaires were already freezing themselves after death. Soon, people who couldn't afford the full procedure would freeze smaller assets: the hands of a painter, the feet of a dancer. It was only a matter of time before every man would have his dick frozen for posterity. The ego lives on.

Harsley now stood behind Kate as she prepared for the first incision. She lifted the scalpel but paused above the sternum. "No," she said.

"What do you mean, no?" Harsley said angrily, advancing. Kate turned to him and gestured at his chest with the scalpel.

"You dragged me in here. I have a right to know why I'm cutting this stiff open for you. At the very least so that I can protect my job if you've finally gone off the deep end."

Harsley clamped his teeth for a moment, staring Kate down. She held her ground and returned his gaze. Eventually, he sighed, put the half cigarette behind his ear, and said, "Fine."

"Talk," Kate said.

Harsley cleared his throat and began walking back and forth across the morgue.

"I went back to Davenport's office tonight. I wanted to give it another once-over."

"Wasn't it already searched? I heard they didn't find anything suspicious. No poison or weapons of any kind."

Harsley stopped in front of the row of metal drawers, seeming to contemplate them.

"That's true. His computer was taken to the station for technological forensics. The only thing left was his bookshelves, some awards for excellence in teaching framed on the wall, and half a cup of coffee. But the desk did have a particular drawer on the bottom right side. It had a lock. It had of course been opened, and its contents were deemed unimportant. Just two books. I thought it was odd for a teacher to lock away some books, seeing as he had several miles of shelving in plain sight. So I took them home. One was a journal. Nothing weird there, just bullshit about advanced mathematics and students. Grace was mentioned a lot. Then I noticed that a few pages had been ripped out. I guess the first guys on the scene thought he'd used it for scratch paper. But the second book was really interesting."

Harsley turned back to Kate. He reached into his coat pocket and produced a small folio bound in black leather.

Nothing was written on the cover. Harsley had stuck a couple of Post-it notes between the pages. He handed it to Kate.

"Is this a Bible or something?" Kate asked.

"That's what I thought at first," Harsley said. "Open it."

Kate opened the book and was stunned. The yellowed pages were inscribed with unintelligible black script. The characters of this unknown language rose and fell jaggedly across the page like waves during a storm. For some reason that Kate couldn't explain, the thought that this language had been scrawled in blood skittered across her mind.

"What language is this?" she asked.

"No fucking clue." Harsley answered walking around Davenport's body with what seemed like a sense of trepidation. "But look at the second page I marked."

Kate flipped to the second Post-it and her stomach contracted. An illustration of a naked man was drawn over the entire left page. He was spread-eagled like the Vitruvian Man, except for his left hand. It was pointing with one finger. West, if his head was north. The skin on his chest had been pulled away on each side like a curtain. Emerging from the chest of this man, like some sort of cocoon, was a creature with many legs and bulbous eyes. Its two forearms looked like scythes reaching above the man's head. Its sweeping wings spread across the entire page, and each wing displayed what looked like crescent moons. Kate looked up at Harsley across Davenport's body. He stared back at her, his jaw hard-set.

"You can't possibly think—" Kate began.

"Just open him up, Steelford. I hope this is all just a waste of time, but something tells me it isn't. Just open the poor bastard up."

Kate had never heard Harsley speak about a victim with pity before. His sudden sympathy scared her. She picked up her scalpel and hesitated above the sternum again. Harsley said, "Come on. You can do this."

There was no trace of sarcasm in his voice. Kate took a deep breath and pressed the blade into the cold flesh. It came apart easily, and for the first time in years Kate felt repulsed by a corpse. She started with the heart and the lungs, taking them out and weighing them. The lungs were normal, but the heart showed signs of distress and tissue damage consistent with a myocardial infarction. She explained all this to Harsley.

"There are poisons out there that do that. Keep looking," he said.

She cut through the fat and muscle of the belly and folded open the sections of flesh. She removed the liver, which looked relatively healthy. Eric wasn't much of drinker in life. The kidneys and the intestines were all normal. She moved onto the stomach.

"Let's see what this guy's last meal was."

She reached over the curling tube of intestine and let out a scream. The tissue moved. Harsley and Kate jumped back, horrified. Something was pushing against the lining of the stomach, making it tremble. Harsley grimaced again and said, "Open it."

Kate's hand shook. She didn't comprehend what was happening. She finished the incision and stepped back. The trembling stopped. Then two black antennae as thin as thread poked their way out of the dead man's stomach. Long, searching legs followed, pulling at the slippery surface of the organ, trying to gain traction. With slow and terrible progress, a green insect crawled out of the dead man's body. It perched on the flap of skin that Kate had pulled back. Its skeletal body was wet, and the wings pressed against its vibrating body. Its two front appendages, like little green daggers, twitched back and forth as if sewing something in the air. Kate and Harsley watched in shock as the praying mantis extended its wings to dry, displaying twin crescent moons on the back. Harsley came back to life first.

"Get a jar, Steelford. And hurl if you need to. I'll be right behind you."

*

Kate stood outside the morgue, shivering under a streetlamp. Harsley came out and lit a cigarette. He offered her one and she took it gratefully. For a moment neither of them spoke, just exhaled smoke in silence. They had found over two dozen mantis eggs in Eric's stomach, each about the size of a jelly bean. A few others had broken open and the resulting dead mantises had been partly broken down by the stomach acid.

"I filed the report for you. We can let the machine take over from here. Let them deal with the bugs."

Kate nodded but said nothing. She continued shivering. Harsley took off his coat and draped it over her shoulders. She let him. She felt like little legs were crawling all over her.

"What the hell was that?" she asked.

Harsley shook his forty-seven-year-old head. His gray hair was tousled by the light wind, and he stared ahead pensively. For a moment Kate thought that he looked like the captain of a ship heading into a storm.

"I don't know, Steelford. But I've got a really bad feeling about it."

Kate looked into the sky. Shining through the dark clouds like a great yellow eye was the sickle of a crescent moon.

DAVID CALBERT

3.

TWELVE THINGS TO DO INSTEAD OF SMOKING CIGARETTES read the poster on the wall of the Underhill Infirmary, where an impromptu "Grief Counseling" center had been established. Underneath a black-and-white photograph of a crushed butt was a colorfully illustrated list of carefully thought-out alternatives: JUMP, SWIM, SMELL, DANCE.

Imogen didn't smoke but began seriously to consider it.

She looked down at her stubby fat fingers and chipped black polish, and frowned. She frowned so often that she couldn't tell anymore when she was frowning and when she wasn't. The perpetually furrowed brow had begun at age thirteen, a spontaneous defense she'd developed while walking through the large, anonymous locker halls of her high school and meeting the inquisitive gazes of her parents at the dinner table. Six years later, it was here to stay.

The door opened behind her and a tall bald man breezed in, flashing a blinding white smile. The top of his head, too, reflected an alarming brilliance as if the metaphorical lightbulb in his brain was real. He couldn't have been over thirty-five; his baldness was the voluntary kind. Imogen wondered whether the Pepto-Bismol-colored shirt he was wearing was also voluntary.

"Hi, Imogen. I'm Chad," he said in a breathy coo, like a shopping mall masseur trying hard to keep up appearances. He used two hands to shake her one, a group hug sort of handshake. Imogen felt more supported already.

"Were you a student of Eric's?" he asked, planting himself in the beige velour La-Z-Boy opposite her.

"Yes."

"It's been a terrible shock. Such a loss for the community."

Imogen twirled the mangy turquoise hair wrap she'd had since her family cruise to Jamaica over the summer. She had trouble responding to platitudes. "Yeah. The whole campus is kinda quiet. No one knows what to do." She trailed off, reluctant to engage Chad's shiny head and the special wisdom he had prepared, and almost forgot why she was there. "But, my roommate—she was one of Eric's students, too—she's having a really rough time."

Chad wore a pained expression, as if cultivating his own brand of menstrual cramps, that encouraged Imogen to keep talking.

"She cries all the time. She can't sleep. She barely touches her food." Imogen waited for this to marinate, then leaned in and lowered her voice conspiratorially: "I think it's affecting her studies."

Chad winced with trained empathy. "Grief is no joke."

"No, it sure isn't. I guess I wanted to know if there was anything I could do to help her."

"Well, she is lucky to have a friend like you, Imogen. I'd be happy to talk to her teachers, let them know she'll need more time for work this semester. Unfortunately, there isn't a whole lot you can do besides what you're already doing. Support her. Let her know you care. Let her know she's not alone. The whole community is grieving right now. We need each other more than ever."

"Right." Imogen felt a horrible, inappropriate giggle rise up her throat, one she would have to apologize for and attribute to nervous laughter. Quickly, she looked at the floor and practiced her own version of Chad's pained face. "But it's also kind of scary. If Eric was murdered—"

"That's not official," he said, straightening and suddenly dour. His area of expertise was apparently very narrow and didn't venture beyond the guidance of a solicitous and simple-minded aunt.

"Not yet, maybe. I know people who have already been questioned by detectives. In which case there's a very good chance the murderer is still here. I mean, he could be anyone. You guys might need to start offering fear counseling."

Chad closed his eyes and took an extended yoga breath. "There are so many heightened emotions after a shock like this."

*

Outside, the sun seared Imogen's fair, quarter-Scandinavian complexion. The other three-quarters were a mutt blend of shanty Irish and unidentified Caucasian. Her mother always said there was some Russian in there somewhere. But unlike Slavic gymnasts and models, Imogen boasted no cheekbones, no angles of any kind, just round, mushy features nurtured on family-style portions of buttered peas and mashed potatoes that could only have sprung from the dregs of some white peasant stock. She had freckles, too, tawny specks that never wiped off, which Imogen hated even when everyone else insisted they were cute.

Squinting in the glare, she traded her black plastic–rimmed specs for prescription Wayfarers. Her eyesight was on a par with most eighty-year-olds'; since she was allergic to contacts, bifocals were a non-negotiable condition of life. Like members of other slighted groups, short people and Canadians, for instance, Imogen could reel off an entire roll call of famous and excellent people who shared the pain and shame of glasses. They were the nobility of her tribe: Woody Allen, Tina Fey, John Lennon, Bill Gates.

Head down, she traversed the grassy expanse, resolute as a donkey, backpack bouncing. On the campus, monuments of learning stood unmoved and unchanged as the litter of students passed through their doors. It was an incongruous match—the stately buildings and the bumbling students, preoccupied with their library crushes and tattoo ideas—yet that was the conventional arrangement.

In the school's popular quad, under a bell tower named for its nineteenth-century founder, small groups huddled in isolation from each other, murmuring and shifting self-consciously. Under the oak tree, hemp kids sat cross-legged, smoking

American Spirits and drawing on each other's arms. They wore strictly earth tones, had forsworn animal products, and appointed status according to how matted and greasy their hair was. But they were a peaceful bunch, and if it hadn't been for their smug self-righteousness, Imogen might have liked them. One of the boys, the greasiest of them all, in a ponytail and Tevas, sat braiding blades of grass and rocking back and forth.

The would-be alpha males, hunched over their preferred table in hoodies and Air Jordans, were quieter than usual and their hand gestures less flamboyant. Even the J. Crew girls seemed less rested and put-together. Imogen noted with some interest that one of the girls' belts didn't match her shoes.

Only the dumpy girls—victims of the "freshman fifteen"—clad in university sweatshirts, pajama bottoms, and Ugg boots, seemed their same old naturally caffeinated selves, undeterred by the brooding menace that had everyone else in a choke-hold. They were seated around some benches, feet up on the tables, stuffing their mouths with microwaveable popcorn and talking loudly enough to be heard across the courtyard. Had their mothers been too nice to them? Had they received one too many trophies for participation, one too many Outstanding Citizen ribbons? Did they still believe they were special? They acted as if they were at their own private sleepover, as if all of college was their personal pizza party. Imogen shuddered, recalling how she had almost become one of them. A year ago, during that first traumatic month of freshman year, they were the only people who were actively nice and inclusive, surely sensing in Imogen one of their own. If it hadn't been for Grace, who alone saw her true potential—the sparkling gem of a personality that deserved better conversations with cooler people—Imogen would assuredly be with them now, wearing cupcake-patterned pajamas in public and laughing at an irritating pitch with popcorn kernels stuck in her teeth.

Warily, she looked around for a familiar face. In the corner she spotted Hannah R. and Marin and Clay, slurping on iced coffees in plastic go-cups.

"Hey," said Imogen.

"Hey," they said in unison.

"What's going on?"

"They made it official," Clay said, looking up from his mangled, tooth-marked straw. "Eric Davenport was murdered."

"Do they know how?"

"They didn't say."

"Obviously, it was poison," said Marin, leaning in to pick a stray crumb off of Imogen's sweater.

"The school's understating the hell out of it," said Hannah R.

"What did they say?"

"They said they would appreciate our full cooperation and if anyone has any information to go straight to Dean Bauer."

Clay shuddered at the mention of the Dean of Norms and Fundamentals, who ruled over all nonacademic aspects of student existence at Underhill.

"I bet it was the janitor who's always lurking around Mansfield. You know, the one with the eye thing." Marin made an ambiguous hand gesture.

"Mar, that's so racist," Clay reproached him.

"Fine, who do you think it was?"

"Bob Shapiro, obviously." Clay flipped the end of his scarf theatrically over his shoulder. "He's held a grudge since he got passed over for tenure, like, a year ago. Or . . . it's one of the late Mr. Davenport's students."

"One of his female students, you mean?" Hannah R. snickered.

"I didn't say nuthin'."

"How's Grace doing?" Marin asked.

"Marin!" scolded Hannah R.

"What did I do now?"

"You're insinuating . . ."

"No, Hannah R., *you're* insinuating. *I* was asking about our dear friend Grace. She's the one that found the poor bastard, isn't she?"

"Who?"

"Grace."

"No, *who*. You should say that she was the one *who* found the poor bastard. Not the one *that* found the poor bastard."

"Thanks for the grammar lesson."

"No problem."

"Well, if you're someone THAT needs to know, it is a problem. But Grace is okay," Imogen said.

"Maybe it *was* Grace," suggested Clay. He pinched his chin with a mock philosophical air. "Food for thought."

"That's really not funny!" Hannah R. pouted and turned to Imogen. "Give her my love, will you?"

*

Imogen made a point of jingling her keys before unlocking the door. This was to alert Grace that she was coming in, which seemed like the polite thing to do.

The room was dark and sour smelling. A Fiona Apple piano ballad played from a laptop resting haphazardly on the floor between an open Snapple and some dirty socks. Imogen hopped over to the window by way of the small islands of clear space among the scattered shoes and food wrappers, library books, and *US Weeklies*. When she pulled up the blind, the whole ugly mess was exposed and made vulnerable like some deep-water creature that was never supposed to see light.

Pictures covered the walls: photographs of Grace and Imogen making funny faces; candid shots; photos of pets; a film still of Winona Ryder and Angelina Jolie in *Girl, Interrupted*; a map of the world with red pins marking where Grace had been, green for Imogen, and purple for where they planned to travel during their proposed summer backpacking tour; a Janis Joplin poster, though neither Grace nor Imogen listened much to her music.

"Grace?" Imogen sat down beside a lump in the bed and tugged gently on the covers. "Can you even breathe in there?"

Grace secured the covers defiantly over her head.

"I went to the counselor at the Health Center." Imogen's voice came out fragile and nervous, like the front line of a doomed siege. "He was a total dope, but he said he could help you get extensions for your classes."

Imogen thought she could hear Grace sniffle under the covers and patted her soothingly. She was prepared to sing a lullaby, if necessary. "I hate to see you like this. Is there anything I can do?"

Grace stirred, poking her bleary head out. "You can leave me alone."

"C'mon. That's not fair."

"Life isn't fair, is it?"

Given Grace's recent unpleasantness, Imogen couldn't say her behavior now was much of a surprise. But it still stung. She, too, had feelings. Was it right that Grace seemed perfectly content to trample all over them? Halfway into a deep, concentrated breath, Imogen shook out of it, alarmed to be cribbing a move from Chad.

"I didn't want to have to go here, but do you really think you mattered to him at all? You were just another easy undergrad. If he hadn't died, you would've been cursing him by now like some scorned woman cliché."

"Are you done yet?" Grace glared with a dark, feral intensity that at once startled Imogen and aroused a bitter passion.

"Be honest. You didn't even like him that much! You just thought an affair with a teacher would make a good chapter in your memoirs!"

"The man is dead!" Grace choked.

Imogen could see that her roommate was truly tormented: her face was pale and gnarled from distress. Taking hold of Grace's arm, stroking it, Imogen pleaded, "I'm sorry.

I didn't mean it. Grace, I love you." She bowed to kiss her hand, but Grace swatted her away like a fly.

"You don't mean that," Imogen said. "I know you don't mean that."

"We've talked about this. It was just a phase! When are you going to get that? I mean, you didn't really think . . . ?" Then—as if noting that Imogen really did think—Grace gave a loud and persuasive groan, plugged up her ears, and thrashed in the sheets.

"But I love you!" Imogen shrieked in a hideous and desperate gesture of allegiance to the big, unfashionable emotions. She didn't care that she was humiliating herself. She was standing up for the truth. She was standing up for love, which was more than Grace could say. Grace was a coward. But Imogen would forgive her this fault in time.

"Well, don't! You disgust me. Okay?"

Imogen felt woozy and unstable like a big cedar trunk when someone had just yelled, "Timber! " Grace had gone too far this time; still, Imogen believed they would look back on this someday as a feisty lover's quarrel. She got up from the bed and turned toward the door, knowing that "space" was in order.

"Good-bye!" Grace shouted and pulled the covers over her face.

Imogen whipped around, nostrils flaring with animal spite. Grace knew her buttons. But she knew Grace's, too, and if she had had one iota less self-control she would have taken Grace's precious little stuffed goat from her childhood and stabbed scissors into it repeatedly. But Imogen had a fair vision of the repercussions, which included Grace requesting a new roommate and never speaking to her again. So she grabbed her backpack instead and the large plastic case on the dresser containing two perfect specimens of praying mantis.

As if she could see through her bedding, Grace added one last cut. "And take your creepy-ass bugs with you! If I see them here again, I'll flush them down the toilet!"

"They're not bugs! They're insects!"

Imogen marched down the hall, cradling the plastic case snugly in her arms, and headed straight for Administration. She was a force to be reckoned with, a woman on a mission. Imogen smiled to herself as an image of Grace wafted through her head, crying and kissing her feet for forgiveness. At the main desk, a wiry woman with yellow skin and too much blush looked up from her computer.

"Can I help you?"

"I'm here to see Dean Bauer," Imogen said.

"Do you have an appointment?"

"No. But I have some information regarding the murder of Eric Davenport."

The secretary became quite alert following this announcement, like a bank teller, Imogen decided, commanded to put the money in the bag or else. She cleared her throat. "Please have a seat. The dean will be with you shortly."

Imogen sat down in the waiting area, feeling triumphant. She gazed into the plastic case on her lap, at the graceful chartreuse slants relaxing under umbrellas of vegetation: it looked like a little paradise. Imogen majored in biology, not owing to any deep-seated passion for organic life but because the subject came easily to her and was preferable to replying, "Undecided," when anyone asked what her major was. Somebody always asked.

Lately, she had experienced a newfound appreciation for life in its entomological microcosm, the no-nonsense power structures and simplified relationships of mate, predator, and prey. It seemed unfair that in humans such instinctual social behavior was repressed and punished, deemed antisocial and squashed before it had time to find its natural expression. The praying mantis didn't have morals because she didn't need them. Why grieve what was natural and necessary? There was no grief counseling in the animal kingdom.

KELSEY JOSEPH

4.

Grace heard the door slam and poked her head out from under the duvet. A whiteboard filled with notes and reminders had crashed to the ground in the wake of Imogen's dramatic exit. Grace sat up, sniffling, wiping her eyes. Her palms came away with wet, dark mascara smudges. She rubbed them on Imogen's scarf, left on the foot of her bed. Alone, finally, she thought. She stretched, scratching her side and yawning, drained from her histrionic performance. Fingering the rubber ropes of her fraying lace thong, Grace flashed back to the last time she had been this tired. That was six months ago, and she had been wearing the same thong. She had gotten it to please Eric.

Grace had sighed with exhaustion back then, her satisfaction having less to do with the orgasm than the man who had given it to her. She sat up against the motel room's chipped fleur-de-lis headboard and ran her fingers through her sweaty hair. "That was incredible, our best yet."

Eric lay completely still, hands arranged perfectly across his chest. Abruptly, he seemed to remember Grace's presence and shifted to his side. He swung an arm over Grace's stomach and aimed a kiss at her cheek. She turned her head at the last second and caught his lips on hers. She gripped his head, pulling him toward her impatiently, hungrily. Eric reciprocated with increasing vigor—until Grace noticed the cold metal of Eric's wedding band on her cheek. She opened her eyes and pulled her mouth from his lips.

"Honey, please," she exhaled. "Can't you remove that thing when you're with me? Put it on the nightstand. Put it in your pocket."

"I'm sorry, but what if I take it off and leave it here? I'm afraid I'll lose it. What if I leave it in my pocket when I do the wash?"

"I doubt *she'd* notice."

He sank back into the cheap, rough sheets. There was a moment of silence.

"What are you thinking about?" Eric asked. He looked to her for an answer, but she wasn't looking at him. She stared straight up at the popcorn ceiling.

"I'm thinking about how Imogen is probably waiting for me. She's always worrying. She's always lecturing me. 'Grace, you're only going to get hurt.' What a nag. God, does she hate you. I swear she's almost jealous of you, or maybe she's just in love with me. I mean I did once walk into our dorm room to find her sniffing my dress."

"You told her?" Eric pinched the skin between his eyes.

"Don't worry. I didn't tell her your name. It's cool. Anyway, I have the right to talk about my relationship with a friend.

Sometimes you don't answer my phone calls and I know it's because you're with your wife. Or when you do answer, you pretend I'm Arjun from your fantasy baseball league. I need to vent."

"I pretended you were someone else only once. You can't make generalizations based on one event. Causation does not connote correlation." Eric shifted into professorial mode.

"Oh please, stop. We're in bed, not the classroom. I'm sick of this deception. I'm tired of being your lie." She took his hands and held them in hers. Her eyes started to water. "I'm in love with you, Eric. And I know you love me. Do what's right. Leave her. Please. I need to know I'm your only woman." She chewed meditatively on a blue Gummy bear.

"Oh, Grace." He wiped away her tears. "I love you, too," he said with a smile.

"Just tell me you're thinking about leaving her. Tell me you have a timetable for leaving her or something. Give me a lie I can believe." Her voice quivered.

"Why change?" Eric sighed. "I thought things were going pretty well."

"Oh you're terrible! You're awful!" Grace cried.

"Let me talk. Why does jealousy have to come into it? What's wrong if I'm in love with more than one person? It doesn't mean I love you any less. I wish you could see that. It's okay to have feelings for multiple people; it's natural." He peeled the quilt off her face. "Honey, I know you've been conditioned to believe in monogamous relationships, but just listen to what I'm saying. I wouldn't mind if you branched out as well."

Grace threw the sheets off her body as if she was overheated, "I don't want anyone else! I want you! Are you . . . are you saying there's someone else besides your wife?"

MADELINE DESSANTI

5.

Grace threw Imogen's scarf at the trash can—the mascara had done worse damage to the puce cashmere than she'd expected. Her aim was off, though, and the scarf landed half-draped over the alarm clock. The digital lights glared 3:00 p.m. through the thin fabric. This was Grace's usual meeting time with Miriam, her advisor. She had been missing their meetings a lot lately, especially since she had mistakenly spilled her guts about Eric. . . .

*

Four months earlier

Miriam Aarons checked her watch: 3:15 p.m. Grace was late. Miriam rubbed her temples. Her advisee was often a few minutes behind schedule, sliding into class with a smile and an excuse. Grace Montoya could be careless, but she didn't forget appointments—that was something Miriam had always liked about her. But this time was different. And, there was that whole paper business. Grace ought to have turned in a short essay discussing Pincus-Witten's theory of post-minimalism and its effect on the moving sculpture. It was a simple assignment, and the class had had plenty of time to complete it. Yet three days had passed since the deadline, and Grace's paper was MIA. Miriam had meant to talk to her before class, but Grace came in ten minutes late. This was supposed to be their make-up meeting.

The knob started to turn, and Miriam looked up from her computer. Grace slipped inside and closed the door quietly behind her.

"Hi. Sorry," she mumbled, setting down her small hemp backpack. She was wearing a leather jacket, miniskirt, and gray tights. A knitted scarf hung from her neck, although it was a warm spring day. Miriam motioned for the girl to sit down.

"What's going on, Grace?"

Grace avoided her gaze. "I don't know."

Miriam sighed. "Yes, you do. You haven't photographed your installation, and I'm missing your post-min paper. I'll have to give you an incomplete if you don't turn in those assignments."

Grace tugged at a hoop earring.

"Look, if you don't understand the material, please tell me. I'm a resource."

"No, like, I get it. There's just been . . . stuff."

Miriam frowned and examined Grace for a moment. "Academic stuff or personal stuff?" she asked.

The girl shifted uncomfortably in her chair. She pulled her knees up to her chest and replied, "Personal, I guess. I really don't know. Sorry, I totally can't talk right . . . I mean, I'm just, like, frustrated, you know?" Grace sniffled and rubbed the stud in her right nostril as her eyes teared up.

Miriam reached for a tissue box she kept for more emotional students. "Would you like to talk about it?" she asked gently. She could always tell when her advisees needed to confide.

Grace shrugged. "I mean, yeah. But I don't know if I can. Like, you might think it's weird, or something. It kinda involves another person, and I don't really have their permission. He— they— don't want me to, like, spread it around. And I totally get that, but I'm still sort of pissed. The situation's pretty fucked," she concluded.

"Ah," Miriam murmured understandingly. "So this is about a guy?"

Grace nodded and put her head on her knees. She said something, but the sound was muffled.

"I'm sorry, I can't hear you."

Then, as if a secret button had been pushed, Grace sat bolt upright and snapped, "Men are pigs!"

Her advisor folded her hands.

"I mean I don't even get it anymore. He likes me, but he's so fucking weird."

"How so?" said Miriam calmly "If you don't mind me asking."

The girl shook her head. "No, it's cool." She smoothed her skirt and began, "Okay, so we'll be, like, really clicking. I mean, really. And just when I'm about to finish—or whatever—he starts talking. About the most random shit! Like, other people he hooked up with, or some article, or some experiment, and he completely ignores me. What the hell is a gambit, anyway? I sort of get it when he yells, 'Storm my castle!' but what the actual fuck? I mean, I have needs, too!"

"Grace," Miriam interjected. "Maybe I'm not the person to talk to about this."

"No, I'm not finished! Then, he'll assign me extra reading— like I'm some sort of a dumb fuck for not getting all his stupid references. Seriously, I don't give a shit about Schrödinger's cat or any of that probability crap."

Miriam's eyes widened. "You're dating a professor? A math professor?" she whispered. There were only three math professors at Underhill. Two were senescent. That left Eric Davenport, a thrilling algebraic buck who'd been involved with another student several years earlier.

Grace crossed her arms and glared back defiantly. "So what if I am?" Then, she began to cry. Miriam was too astonished to offer more tissues.

"Please, don't tell anybody!" the girl moaned, mascara running down her face. "Don't we have, like, a prof-student confidentiality agreement?"

"Grace, what he's doing is wrong. It needs to be reported."

"No! That will totally fuck up his career!"

"Well, under the circumstances, it's only right," Miriam said grimly. She paused. "Will you continue to see him?"

Grace shrugged. "Yeah, probably. I mean, he's weird, but I'm really into him. I don't know." Suddenly, she reached across the desk and grabbed Miriam's arm. "As a friend, though, what would you advise? Please."

Miriam pressed her lips together and eyed her student thoughtfully. The girl looked so pale, so desperate. What should she do now? she thought. Then, the answer came to her, and she smiled.

"Turn in your paper, Grace. Then, we'll talk."

JESSYE HOLMGREN-SIDELL

6.

The scent of magnolia blossoms hovered stubbornly. Already, the early morning air was like Harsley's great aunt Ruby's parlor curtains: suffocating, perfumed, fermenting, and crawling with bugs.

Harsley and Carl strode up the Hurst Green sidewalk, their feet scuffing on caulked cement cracks. "She's at 4545 Tapioca Lane," Harsley said, less to Carl than to himself. He glanced again at the crinkled scrap paper, now smeared with sweat in his fist, where he'd scribbled the address the late Professor Eric Davenport shared with his wife. On occasions of potential homicide, Harsley usually made straight for the spouse. He could list a score of great reasons to turn your lawfully wedded into your dearly departed, commencing hypothetically with sex and money.

The former more than the latter brought thoughts of Lisa to mind. Harsley imagined his mangled body, discovered days later after the deed by the postman, who would have rung and rung the doorbell. After years of helping Harsley crack his cases, Lisa would know exactly how to get away scot-free. He

imagined her sweet-talking beat cops in the midst of a rum-
mage sale on her front lawn, nonchalantly selling the pickax
she had used to hack him apart for a quick thirty bucks.

But a pickax would be sloppy, and Lisa hated mess. During
the good years of their marriage, she had joked that she'd use an
icicle if she wanted to kill him. Then she and Ronnie the insurance man would slip away to Tijuana, drink from a margarita
fountain, and fuck while a mariachi band serenaded them.

Harsley was jolted back to reality. They had stopped
walking, and the mailbox before them read 4545—DAVENPORT in
flowery script.

"This interview's gonna be a bitch," he said. Harsley was in
no mood to comfort a sobbing widow, sticky with sorrow and
snot. She would no doubt be middle-aged and sagging—there
had to be a reason why Davenport would stray to that tight little
jail bait—and at this hour of the morning, Mrs. Davenport would
probably be arrayed in a slovenly bathrobe and curlers. Harsley
shook the boner-shrinking imagery from his mind's eye.

He shielded his gaze from the glaring sun, appraising the
Davenport residence. The house rose up from a large manicured lawn, a stainless, virgin-white behemoth with bay windows and several rows of yellow tulips flanking the perimeter
like the queen's guard at Buckingham Palace. The grass had
been freshly watered by automatic sprinklers; its saturated,
glinting green and unnatural velvet appearance made it seem
more like an outdoor rug than organic flora. All was utterly
pristine, even nauseating. Harsley regarded the topiary
shaved into abstract shapes. He assumed they were meant to

be tastefully elegant, but to him it all looked like decapitated poodles.

Carl checked his watch and looked about him, as though growing bored. His forte lay more in people than landscapes. He knew he had the approachable demeanor of a Labrador retriever and used it to his advantage with suspects, inducing them to let their guard crumble. He cleared his throat. "Shall we?"

Harsley grunted affirmatively and strode past Carl, neglecting the pathway for a grassy hypotenuse. His shoes dug into the wet soil. Carl followed on the cobblestones. The doorbell chimed like church bells when Harsley jabbed it. From somewhere inside the house, a shrill dog's bark echoed as if from underground.

"Who are these people—they think they're friggin' deities?" Carl murmured, eyeing the door's Pantheon-like plaster pillars.

"Don't say 'friggin', Baker; it's unbecoming to your manhood," Harsley chastised his assistant. "Use real profanity like a big boy."

The hardwood door opened slowly, and the detectives straightened their posture. They stared into the foyer, eyes drifting in empty space.

"Yes?" said a soft female voice.

Harsley and Carl both looked down. Just below their line of vision stood a diminutive woman, Puerto Rican or Dominican by the look of her bone structure, Harsley thought. Barely breaking five feet, the maid was bedecked in a crisp black blouse and white apron, ornately frilled at the hem. All was meticulously buttoned and starched painfully stiff. Harsley lit a cigarette.

"Err, yes, hello. I'm Sergeant Baker, and this is my partner, Detective Harsley." Carl discretely flashed his badge. "We're here to speak with Mrs. Davenport, about the . . . , uhh, unfortunate passing of her husband,"

The maid stared blankly up, eyes darting back and forth between the two men. "Mrs. Davenport? She . . . she not home," the maid chirped nervously.

Suddenly, the dog's barking began again and a Cavalier King Charles Spaniel shot past the door and through Harsley's legs. The detectives watched as the tiny thing darted into the front yard, yipping wildly. Carl made an impulsive start to catch the dog, but just as it neared the sidewalk, they heard a quiet electric zap, and the dog collapsed.

"Is . . . is it okay?" Carl said staring, confused and horrified.

"Invisible fence, suburban canine reality," Harsley said simply, turning back to the Davenport maid. He looked at her over his sunglasses. "When exactly do you expect her back, ma'am?"

The maid hesitated for a moment then stepped aside. "Please, come in."

Carl wiped his feet on the doormat, and the two stepped into a grand oval vestibule. A mahogany table stood center stage, waxed and buffed to a reflective shine. It supported an enormous vase of condolence lilies and crème roses. The walls were an immaculate eggshell-white; a small red love seat and blue rug were the only two Mondrian splashes of color, so precise they seemed painted into the scene.

"Wait here one moment please, sirs," the maid murmured, and disappeared through a pair of French doors.

Harsley meandered around the room. He glanced at his reflection in a large Art Deco pier glass, smoothed back his thinning hair, and moved to an accent table, which sported more funereal flowers. A turned-down photograph caught Harsley's eye; he picked up the heavy silver frame and examined the picture. Barbie and an aging Ken beamed up at him through the glass—Eric and his wife. Harsley was surprised; she was a gorgeous platinum blonde. It was clearly their wedding photo: Eric sported an expensive tuxedo; Mrs. Davenport wore her white gown like a second skin. The lace hugged her ample chest deliciously, and she smiled a Colgate smile. Harsley wondered just how much of her was bleached besides her teeth. The couple hugged each other, not too tight, formal, for the photographer. Both looked unaccustomed to the shiny new rings on their left hands; Eric's was especially ostentatious. Carl looked over his shoulder.

Harsley rubbed the photo's glass with his thumb. "This is the only dusty thing in the entire room." He raised his fingers to show Carl. He flipped the frame over. "The front side is dirty—the backside is clean. Rosalita over there must dust every day, no?"

"Sure," Carl agreed, resenting his partner's off-color racial tag. "But I doubt she moves anything around."

"Exactly. So this picture's been turned down for a while now."

The maid reappeared, her quick, light step echoing around the vaulted room. The spaniel, doing fine, trotted behind her. She handed Harsley a thick pamphlet and hovered at his elbow. "Mrs. Davenport away, maybe come back tonight or tomorrow," she said. "Artichoke"—she gestured with her chin to the

dog—"has show next week. Missus never misses show." Carl
and Harsley looked down at the dog, then back to the pamphlet.

The cover displayed several African children with dis-
tended stomachs and saucer-big eyes staring out from the page
with confused and hungry expressions. Arms snuggling two of
them, there was Mrs. Davenport, dressed in tight beige khaki
and smiling brightly. Harsley opened the pamphlet and read,
"Bridging nations, feeding families, healing with hygroscopy,"
before the text continued with the pitch: "Bring new purity to
those in need. Herbal colon hydrotherapy: a proven method
to reinvigorate the body and soul. Help wash away suffering,
inside and out! Carry colonics to Africa! Conference Summit
to be held on the S.S. *Queen Aphrodite*, destination St. Bart's."

Harsley looked up at the maid then over to Carl in disbelief.
"She's . . . on a colonic cruise?"

The maid frowned at his tone and reached for the pamphlet.

"If they're starving, why do they need their colons cleaned?"
Harsley avoided the maid's outstretched grasp and tucked the
pamphlet into his pocket.

The maid looked frustrated and defeated. "Mrs. Davenport
will be back soon. Thank you for coming," she said shortly, and
ushered Harsley and Carl out.

The door slammed behind them.

"Well, that was a bust," Carl said, disappointed.

Harsley retrieved the pamphlet and admired the grieving
spouse's body-hugging, low-cut safari shirt. "I'll say."

SASHA PEZENIK

7.

Two blocks away from the brilliant intellectual doings at Underhill College, Cathleen O'Conlan sat in bed and picked her cuticles, a habit she knew her husband found revolting. Fortunately, his back was turned and his light was out. Cathleen, however, was familiar with insomnia these days.

"Hank."

Hank twitched. "Mrmphhhgh."

Cathleen reached over and flicked on his light. "I think we should send Michael to see someone."

Hank rolled over, pulling most of the sheets with him. "Cathleen," he sighed with a tinge of annoyance. Her late-night ramblings were starting to remind him of his mother, a neurotic lady with too much time on her hands.

"I know you think it's important for him to deal with this on his own, but he's only fourteen. Janine recommended someone who specializes in kids his age." The ceiling fan above their bed whirled slowly, as though it were spinning through hummus.

"Not now," Hank replied with a sigh.

"It's obvious that you prefer Simon, and Michael is catching on. He's going through a lot. And he's sensitive. I think about that Professor Davenport and how much he meant to Mick, and . . . well, you just brush it off. The chess club was his only outlet, and that man took him under his wing." Cathleen wiped tears from her eyes.

"Cathleen, calm down. You're blowing this out of proportion," Hank said.

"I can't help but worry."

Hank turned away and pulled the covers back over his body. He always slept without trouble.

Down the hall, Michael studied Eric Davenport's papers with a flashlight. Simon tossed and turned in his bed across the room. Michael didn't care if he was keeping his brother up. There were more important things to do. Simon would have to deal with it.

"I can't sleep with that fucking light on, Mick," Simon whined. These days, both of the boys used at least one curse word in every sentence. This is our way of defining our independence as young men, Michael thought.

"I don't give a shit," Michael spat back. He handled the papers with great care, as if they were in danger of disintegrating. He was proud that Davenport entrusted him with such documents. Michael wondered if the man knew he was going to die.

"What the hell are you reading anyway?" Simon asked.

"Just some papers."

"Can I see?"

"No fucking way," said Michael. The paper was stained with coffee and smelled musty like Davenport's office. Most of the pages consisted of mysterious equations. Michael admired how elegant they looked. Within the pages, he found a map of the college campus. The prestigious college near his home had served as his playground for as long as he could remember. He preferred its winding paths and Tudor buildings to the park that was a short bike ride away. Michael hadn't found much use for the map until he saw that its layout was reversed, as though Underhill's reflection had been captured in blueprint. As if the man who drew it had been looking through a mirror.

"Turn the damn light off, Mick." Simon was at the end of his rope. It was now past midnight.

"Over my dead body."

"I'll call Mom up here, you chode."

"No, you won't."

"Oh, yeah?" Simon's bellow seemed to shake the whole house. Michael irrationally feared the vibrations of his brother's roar would shatter the pages in his lap. He buried his head between his knees and awaited the inevitable echo of his mother's footsteps. He switched the flashlight off and tossed it under his bed. He tucked the documents under his pillow, as if he could absorb their content in his sleep. The door creaked open, and the light from the hall slowly illuminated his figure under the duvet.

"Boys?" their mother asked.

"Mick was keeping me up with his flashlight. He's reading all that crap the dead professor gave him," Simon reported. "He wouldn't turn it off."

"Mick, it's late. Time for sleep." Her footsteps sounded heavy on the hardwood floor as she made her way back down the hall. Michael decided to take his business to the closet.

Michael sat on the floor among his dirty clothes. Laundry was a responsibility that came with age, but Michael found it too time-consuming. He was grateful for the lightbulb that dangled from the ceiling. The answer to Davenport's murder has to be in these papers somewhere, he thought. Their edges were jagged as if they'd been torn from a notebook. The bulb flickered above his head.

*

Michael and Davenport had met in the professor's office every week for a game of chess. Michael's opponents from the neighborhood didn't have much skill and were easy to beat. Davenport took it upon himself to make sure the boy was properly challenged. Michael reveled in the idea of spending time with a college professor; it affirmed his precocious self-image. During their meetings, Davenport often told Michael stories from his own childhood. Tales of growing up in New England when a burger cost seventy-five cents sounded better to Michael than the reality he faced. Michael often tried to calculate Davenport's age and found himself obsessing over how many years the man had left. Davenport never mentioned his other students, as if he knew it might make Michael jealous.

The last time they met, Davenport lost. This was remarkable, because the professor never let his student win. He said that an unearned victory was meaningless. He leaned back in his cushioned chair with his eyes set on his bookshelves. The wood that supported the books was bowed from their weight. Michael threatened Davenport's rook to see if his mentor was paying attention. A moment later, he captured the rook.

"Sorry, my mind's sort of elsewhere today," Davenport said.

Michael responded with an understanding smile. Just as he put his jacket on to leave, Davenport stopped him and inquired if he'd feed the praying mantis. Back home, Michael had a few books on praying mantises that Davenport lent him. Michael was now an expert on the creature. Eric sat silently as Michael dropped a grasshopper into the carnivore's glass cage. He watched as she caught her prey between her front legs.

"The praying mantis is a creature of rituals," Davenport said. He looked through his desk drawer and handed the boy a sheaf of papers held together with a black paper clip. "Stash these away for me."

"Sure, what for?"

"Safekeeping. I tend to lose things I shouldn't." Davenport chuckled as Michael made his way out. "Michael," Davenport stopped him. He hesitated for a moment, "I'll see you next week, kiddo."

*

A transparent sheet of drawing paper peeked out of Michael's pile. The lightbulb flickered again, threatening to burn out. The waxy paper was filled with a series of lines. In the bottom right-hand corner was a hand-drawn compass rose. Michael placed the transparent paper over the backward layout of the campus. His heart raced as he realized that together, the fragile pages illustrated a network of . . . something—wires or pathways—superimposed onto the school's quads. But no such passages existed. Then Michael realized that if they weren't over the school, they must be under. They were tunnels. And that was where the solution to the mystery of Davenport's death had to be. With these pages, Michael was sure he could uncover the killer. He wouldn't waste time sleeping that night. Michael quickly packed a bag and prepared to embark on a night of investigation.

*

"He's having a hard time. We're looking into therapy," Cathleen said as she and Hank waited with Detective Harsley for Michael to return from Hurst Green Junior High that afternoon. The man had arrived ten minutes earlier, announcing that their son's name was listed in the dead professor's calendar.

Harsley rolled his eyes, "All right, so how close were they?" He sipped coffee that Cathleen had offered. It was a police principle: never refuse a beverage.

"Oh, not that close." Hank shrugged dismissively.

"No, they were quite close, I think. Well, he spent time with him most weeks after chess club. I thought it was sweet," Cathleen said.

"It would be helpful if I could discuss this with your son. But anyhow, have you noticed any changes in his behavior?" Harsley asked.

"He snuck out last night." Cathleen said. "It's just not like him, he's a good son."

"Honey, that was Simon," Hank intervened. "I told you, he's got that girlfriend. I saw him climb out the window. It was Simon."

"They're identical twins," Cathleen explained to Harsley, "but I was sure it was Michael. I heard him sneaking back in when the sun was coming up. We were going to confront them about it today."

"Would your other son, the twin, have anything to do with Davenport?" Harsley asked.

"Oh, no. He was never much of a chess player. And he hates math." Cathleen looked to Hank for validation.

"Thanks. It's been great talking to you folks. But it would be a lot more productive if I could just talk to your son." Harsley was losing patience.

Michael walked through the front door, pale and bleary-eyed from a day at school after a night of sleepless exploration.

"Honey, this is Detective Harsley. He's here to ask you a few questions," Cathleen said. She pulled a chair out for him. Harsley lit a cigarette. The family stared for a moment: no one had ever smoked in their house before. Michael sat, and his parents left the room. He hated them for abandoning him in such a situation. Michael felt the blood rush to his face.

"All right, it's Michael, correct?" Harsley asked. He sifted through a stack of manila folders spotted with multiple stains. Here a coffee; there a jelly donut.

"Yes," Michael affirmed, surprised by how disorganized the detective appeared. He pictured the man obsessing over these scraps of evidence late at night.

"Your mother tells me that you and Davenport were close. But I knew that because your name came up in our investigation. Tell me about the last time you saw him."

"In his office. We met privately after chess club. He said I wasn't being challenged enough. I found out he was dead three days later." Michael tried to decipher the notes that Harsley jotted in his notebook.

Harsley flicked a speck of ash from his pant leg. "Did anything seem strange, or did he say anything the last time you met?"

"No."

Harsley's reading glasses sat low on his nose, and his naked eyes deflated Michael's lie. "Listen kid, this is serious. If you don't tell the truth, there could be a lot of issues on our end. You can take your time, but I need details about the last time you saw Professor Davenport."

"Well, he did seem a little . . . upset. He didn't say much."

Harsley peered at the boy from above the frame of his glasses. Michael hated it when adults did this.

Michael continued with a quiver in his voice, "He asked me to hold onto some papers."

"Did he say why?"

"Safekeeping."

"I'll need those, Michael. Where are they?"

Michael picked up his backpack from the floor beside his chair. The pages were damp and sticky from a leftover tuna sandwich that had been aging beneath a copy of *Julius Caesar*. He surrendered the documents.

"Did Davenport say anything to you about what's in these pages?" Harsley asked.

"No."

"All right. Almost done. Your mother mentioned that you—or your brother—snuck out last night."

Michael rubbed his clammy hands against his jeans to dry them. "Yes," he replied.

"Did it have to do with Davenport?"

"I don't know . . . kind of. There's a map in there that he gave me. And it shows tunnels under the school. I wanted to check them out."

Harsley placed a recorder in front of Michael. When he pressed the red Record button, the click seemed to echo. "Did you?" Harsley asked.

Michael's heartbeat reverberated in his ears. "Yes, I left my house a little after midnight. The entrance to the tunnels was outside the building where Davenport's office is . . . was. The map was written backward, so it's kinda hard to tell where things are. But there's a weird part of the building that is only a few feet high and about this long"—he gestured at the table where they were sitting—"that I asked Davenport about. I thought it was part of the basement. But he just laughed when I asked, said there was no basement. Last night I didn't think I'd be able to get in. But I did."

"How?"

"Well, the entrance is disguised as a sewer. It didn't smell when I moved the big metal plate. And I could see the ground when I shined my flashlight, so I just went down this ladder bolted to the side of the hole."

"Did you see anything?"

"It was dark. I was afraid to get really lost, even with the map. It seems like you really have to know your way around in order to find a way out. At one point I heard voices."

"Yes?"

"So I followed them."

"Yes?" Harsley leaned forward, and his excitement made Michael feel courageous.

"And then there was music. Creepy slow music, like a horror movie. At the end of one tunnel there was an opening blocked with metal bars. That was where it was coming from. But I couldn't get through and figured it was filtering down the pipes from the dorm up above."

"Anything else? Anything else at all?"

"That's it. The light was dim." Michael replied. He was relieved to see Harsley click off the recorder and gather up his notebook and Davenport's papers. Michael wanted to ask how the man had been killed and how much pain he might have felt, or maybe what his body looked like, but he was sure that Harsley took his detective work seriously.

MATTIE HAGERTY

8.

In high school, Clay had liked being tall and skinny. He dressed primarily in black, with the exception of a purple, red, or green handkerchief he hung out his back pocket. He smoked American Spirit cigarettes, listened to vinyl, and took one-minute showers so that the paint stains from art class would stay on his knuckles and make him look like a true artist. He got laid, on average, biweekly.

But everyone at Underhill was tall and skinny, everyone wore black, and everyone had been that semi-outcast hipster simultaneously avoided and worshipped in high school. Worse, everyone was gay, or trying. Even Clay's queerness wasn't queer anymore. He felt duped and resolved to figure out how to be *the* tallest, skinniest, blackest—no, that's not right, is it?—gay artist around. But painting was on its way out anyway, so he decided to take a writing class. Even though he overheard doomsday preachers ranting about the demise of literacy and respect for the "page"—said in an almost-British accent—just about every time he sat down for a meal at the cafeteria, he thought there was something sexy about words, and sex would never go out of style.

Writing was also better for him because painting required a certain amount of skill. Anyone could write.

The first day in his fiction workshop had been rather alarming. When he entered the small room, lit by a lamp so dim he thought the school had invented a five-watt bulb for proper ambience, he found himself staring at a table of would-be writers, all armed with black moleskins and elaborate fountain pens. The boy across from him, who was wearing what appeared to be a rug turned sideways with a slit cut for his head to pop through, was sporting a glass pen and a bottle of ink. He caught Clay staring at it and said, "Blown. From Italy. Venice, Contellini Studio."

The window flew open and a small, squirrely girl came rocketing through, leaping across two empty chairs and sinking into the third one. "Sorry, guys," she grinned. "Method acting. You know how it goes." She performed an incredibly fake and deliberate eye twitch and then continued. "We're working on this new neoclassical interpretation of *Othello*. Desdemona meets Cat Woman meets Judith Butler."

"That sounds radical," chimed Lex, the girl two seats from Clay, as she raised her arms to stretch, revealing a nest of armpit hair. Lesbians, Clay thought with a sigh, noting her seemingly contradictory see-through blouse that hung almost to the nipples that protruded from the gauzy material. Where did the good old seventies dykes go? Bring back the shaved heads, the motorcycles, the spiked belts! It was an exhausting business, trying to figure out how to talk to these strange twenty-first-century specimens.

Now, five months in, the class had followed through on the eccentric professor's assignment: write a group novel. Each person take a chapter and run with it.

"I want blood, I want social commentary, I want deans having orgies with transsexual security guards, I want hover crafts and the reincarnation of Tutankhamun!" the professor had practically yelled during the first class, gesticulating wildly. All of the students except Clay and the weasel-like boy next to him named Ben had nodded seriously, scribbling notes in their moleskins and then staring blissfully into space.

"Gum?" Ben asked, unclasping his cape to drape over his chair and sitting down next to Clay.

"What flavor?" Clay replied, not bothering to look up from his doodles. He was dog-tired. The night before a couple had decided to break up outside his window despite his pathetic pleas for them to take their whimpers, promises to remain friends, and loud kissing noises elsewhere.

"Any!"

"What do you mean?"

"I mean, I have every flavor of gum. Try me." Ben grinned. There was a piece of lettuce caught between his two front teeth. Clay grimaced and looked away. "No thanks."

Gregorio (born Greg) sat down across the round table and coughed. "Hey, Clay," he murmured in the gravely voice he had been working on for months. Clay sighed. Gregorio had been trying to blow him since the fall, but Clay just wasn't into Gregorio's tattoo of the stress and un-stress marks of a line of dactylic heptameter even though Gregorio claimed it was a much misunderstood meter scheme. "*You* try writing in it sometime," Gregorio had said sulkily when Clay snorted at the explanation of the small *u*'s and dashes.

"I'd rather eat from the vegan section of the cafeteria for the rest of my life," Clay replied.

"It's the meter-scheme of a true artist," Gregorio declared, his voice whiny. "It makes you slow down and really think about things before you say them. I've been working on a poem for three years now."

"How long did the one before that take?" Lex asked.

Gregorio blinked. "This is my first. What, you think I could write in dactylic heptameter *before* I was fifteen?"

*

Dick Dupont, the professor, entered, and the class hushed immediately. Clay imagined that Dick came from some tragically common Midwestern family (father who went to trade school, remains 80 percent faithful to his once 90 percent pretty wife, takes joy in drinking Pabst Blue Ribbon, and has some strange hobby, like tinkering with old wristwatches or collecting nineteenth-century horseshoes) but had married out of it to a wealthy French academic he met in college, taking her surname as a way of erasing his beginnings. When Aireka, the squirrely method-acting girl, had raised her hand and asked whether he was related to the founders of the Dupont Corporation, Dick wrinkled his bulb-like nose and winced. Clay was sure Dick had thought "Dupont" had the ring of great French intellectual names such as Pascal or Descartes and hadn't realized that it was in fact one of the most famous French-American names around, recognized not for philosophy or literature but for the huge chemical company that developed Lycra.

"All right, guys. What did you think?" Dupont asked, ruffling the chapter-of-the-week in the air.

Clay looked down at his copy. Gregorio's name stared smugly back up at him in American Typewriter font. Of course Gregorio would type in that font, Clay thought with disgust. The chapter opened with a whimsical, Dedalus-like character—who was described as having the same thick eyebrows and chipped tooth that Gregorio sported—accidentally eating an ancient Mayan opiate and ending up naked in a cleaning cupboard.

"Now, I had asked for a bit of social commentary. To broaden the scope of our piece, you know?" Dupont continued. "What are we saying about America by having a drugged up teenager rant about hoof-and-mouth disease only to end up naked on a box of Windex?"

"Hmmm," murmured Lex.

"Well, you know, like, maybe it's talking about minorities and like, minimum wage, and like, janitors, you know?" one of the perpetually stoned boys across the table said.

"Or, like, cows, and vegetarianism and shit," one of his friends added.

"Janitors?" Dupont asked, still focused on the first boy.

"The cleaning closet, man," the kid replied.

Gregorio smirked proudly. "Exactly."

"That's all very well," Lex cut in, "but I really find your use of the word 'vessel' in the third paragraph quite triggering. It calls to mind Magdalene—as you know, the sacred vessel—and for the rest of the piece I couldn't get away from reading everything as a patriarchal hetero-normative diatribe."

Gregorio sniffed lightly and pretended to write something down.

A willowy girl three seats to the left of Clay sat upright and adjusted her papers until they were all perfectly aligned before speaking. "The other itsy-bitsy problem is that the whole chapter takes place somewhere entirely different than the rest of the story and doesn't have any of the same characters," she began shyly. Gregorio's eyes filled with tears. "But that can easily be fixed!" she squeaked as Gregorio thrust his chair backward and fled the classroom.

"Oh dear," she wailed, her own eyes brimming over, and stood to follow him. She brushed her stack of papers as she grabbed her handkerchief and was halfway to the door before she scampered back, lined the papers up perfectly again, and then rushed after Gregorio.

Dupont let out a long, loud sigh. "Okay. Let's talk bigger problems," he said, running a hand through his thick salt-and-pepper hair. "We are ten chapters in, and each and every one of you has created a new character, only to put them through an exotic and often appalling sexual experience and then kill them in an even more grotesque manner."

The class nodded sagely. Clay rubbed his eyes. He had yet to write a chapter and was not looking forward to the task.

"Now, how could a detective—which we don't have yet, I might add—possibly follow all of these thus-far disconnected crimes to one perpetrator and one motive?"

The class was silent for a moment. Eventually Pan (who had changed her—his?—name from Wendy upon arriving at Underhill) said, "What if, like, the detective followed the trail of the orgies?"

"Do orgies leave a trail, Pan?" Dick replied.

"I mean, it depends."

"What if the murderer is an alien, or a dragon, or something?" Ben piped up. His eyes widened in excitement. "Or an enormous bug!"

"Ew, no," Larissa broke in from the other side of the round table. She finished rearranging her headdress and then continued. "There are already enough bugs on campus with all those stupid praying mantises."

"Yeah, what's up with that?" stoned boy asked.

"Friends, let's try and stay on topic," Dupont interrupted.

"Can I have a cig, prof?" Heathcliff asked.

Dick rummaged around in his pocket and slid a gold foil-tipped Sobranie across the table to Heathcliff, who pulled out a flask-sized Zippo and lit the cigarette.

"At least open the window," Aireka complained.

"I need a drink," Sera moaned.

"Here, have some of mine," Lex offered, handing Sera her Scotch.

"Writing is, like, stressful," Pan sighed.

"At least we already have a publishing deal," Lex commented.

"True," Pan replied.

The class fell into silence for a moment, hushed by the cigarettes lit up around the table like fireflies at dusk.

Through the smoke, Clay heard Dupont addressing him. "Clay? What do you think? I was hoping you would write the next chapter."

"I don't know, Dick," Clay replied. Someone opened the window and the air cleared a bit. "I feel like it's a little strange to be writing a murder mystery, given what's going on right now."

"You mean, like, in Syria?" Pan said with a knowing nod.

"What? No. What?" Clay shook his head, frowning. "What the fuck are you talking about? I mean Davenport."

"Ohhh," Pan cooed.

"What does civil war have to do with murder mysteries, anyways?" Clay said, still extremely annoyed. What was wrong with these people?

"All those deaths," Pan murmured, gazing dramatically out the window.

"Jesus." Clay reached out to take the Scotch from Sera. Sera watched it go with a sad but passive look.

"I know!" Heathcliff said, smoke billowing out his nostrils. "What if all the people who are killed were in a writing class together. What if that's the link?"

"Hmmm," Dupont murmured. "That could work. They *are* all students."

"That's, like, sooo meta," Pan enthused.

"But what would be the motive?" Clay asked.

Heathcliff's eyes glowed brighter than the tip of his cigarette. "They were all writing a book together. About something they shouldn't. . . ."

REBECCA SHEPARD

9.

When Imogen opened the door to her dorm room, Grace was waiting. The only light in the narrow room came from Imogen's desk lamp. Grace had thrown a red scarf over it, ostensibly to create a romantic mood. But in reality the ghostly red light transformed every object in the room, especially the terrarium between their two beds, into a hellish installation, and the only feeling that could justifiably be inferred was rage.

Grace pounced as soon as Imogen entered. She grabbed Imogen by the shoulders and shoved her against the door, slamming it shut. Before Imogen could shout in surprise, she felt Grace's mouth latch onto her own, her teeth and her tongue pressed hungrily against her. Hands moved as if to disassemble her, one undoing the clasp of the belt around her dress, the other gripping her throat to hold her in place. Imogen was frightened, but she responded to Grace's rough caresses. Hips bucked and knees buckled under a tidal wave of arousal. Imogen inhaled Grace's scent, was made dizzy by the intoxicating mix of sweat and lavender perfume. And she could smell something else, something that clouded her capacity for logic, leaving only a primal desire to be ravaged.

Grace peeled Imogen's dress over her head with the dexterity of a taxidermist skinning a moose. They were both naked in seconds, sweaty and panting, Grace eyeing Imogen intently, her eyes catching the room's red glow. Amid the rush of blood and hormones, one sober thought managed to surface.

"Grace," Imogen whispered as her roommate bit down slowly on her collar bone, causing her to wince before continuing, "Grace, you know I want to, how I feel. But, Davenport, you're grieving. . . . I don't want to take advantage."

Grace's fingers slid between Imogen's legs, slick and nimble, erasing any sober thoughts. Grace stumbled back into the redness of the room, coming to rest on the edge of her bed and sitting with her legs splayed. The small tuft of her pubic hair became the hypnotic center of the room to Imogen, a powerful black hole in the center of this carmine galaxy.

"Get on the floor," Grace said. Imogen fell to her knees in a trance. Her skin, in the absence of Grace's caresses, ached for them again. She felt a deep, pulsing itch at her very core, a red coal that Grace had stoked until it was white hot.

"Crawl to me," Grace hissed, her wicked smile twisting into a snarl. Imogen hesitated before the subjugating demand, and for a brief second she wondered if she'd been drugged. Her head was spinning.

"Do it," Grace commanded, and the desire overpowered Imogen as she fell to her hands and knees and crawled across the stained industrial carpet that covered the floor of the dorm room. Grace entwined her fingers in Imogen's hair and pulled her closer.

"Now, let's have some fun," Grace said, and Imogen was lost in the tumult.

*

Afterward, they lay in Grace's bed, naked but not touching. Imogen had her back to Grace to hide the fact that her eyes were wet. Grace drummed her fingers on her own bare chest and stared at the terrarium next to her. She watched the thin green mantises move about their enclosure, hiding along the leafy branch Imogen provided to simulate their natural habitat. Imogen could feel Grace's fidgety movements through the stiff mattress cover, the thick plastic kind that colleges buy to avoid bedbugs. Grace seemed to thrum with energy; Imogen could almost hear her vibrate. After sex, Imogen felt sobered, drained, and a little nauseous. It was like coming down from a cocaine high. The drying of sweat and Grace's saliva left her cold and covered in gooseflesh.

Imogen thought back to the first time that she and Grace had hooked up. It was earlier in the year, before Davenport. It was before either of them had met Hannah R., Marin, and Clay, before they'd met anyone. They drank two bottles of wine while watching *Breaking Bad* on Grace's computer, hands gradually inching toward each other. The sex that night had been light and cheerful; Grace giggled throughout the whole event. Not like tonight. There was no evidence that Grace had the capacity for such sweet savagery, an intensity that scared Imogen.

"Grace," Imogen said, "I'm sorry."

"For what?" Grace replied curtly. She sounded distracted, and when Imogen looked over she saw Grace staring intently at the terrarium. A mantis was holding a recently caught cricket in its sharp front legs, chewing its head off with its lighting quick mandibles.

"I don't know," Imogen said. "Everything feels weird."

"I'm sorry," Grace said, but the words sounded hollow. "You know, praying mantises bite off the head of their lovers right after coitus," Grace said with suddenly greater interest.

"Yeah, I know, it's my major." Imogen started to rise from the bed, but Grace's hand shot out and grabbed her wrist, holding her still. It wasn't loving; it was predatory.

"How durable are they?" Grace asked. She still didn't look at Imogen, but her hand held tightly. It gave Imogen chills.

"What do you mean 'durable'?" Imogen asked. She suddenly wanted very much to leave the room, to leave Grace. She realized that her heart was beating very fast and she had trouble getting enough air in her lungs to speak evenly.

"Are they waterproof?" Grace asked.

"I suppose. Most insects have a protective exoskeleton. Considering their size, insects can perform acts of amazing strength and endure extreme climates. I guess that includes water." Imogen tried to subtly free her wrist, but Grace's fingers were like iron. The nails dug into Imogen's flesh, but she was too afraid to feel the pain.

Grace smirked and said, "No pink underbelly for these Amazon warriors. What about acid?"

Imogen was getting dizzy again. Everything began to feel surreal and she wondered if she had somehow drifted into a dream while lying next to Grace. Then she felt Grace's nails piercing her skin and knew she was awake.

"Acid? What do you mean?"

"Like stomach acid," Grace clarified.

Suddenly, a memory hit Imogen. Clay and his chewed up straw, saying that Davenport was murdered. Marin flicking crumbs off of her sweater saying that it must have been poison.

"Grace, I have to go. I need to get something from the library."

Grace said nothing, but she released her grip. Imogen quickly dressed and fled. She wandered around in a daze, nausea resurfacing along with an idea, a horrible idea that she couldn't, didn't want to believe until she found herself knocking on Dean Bauer's door for the second time that week.

The Dean of Norms and Fundamentals, a category including any events that occurred in residences or dining halls or ball fields or anyplace besides a classroom, sat in an executive wire-frame chair that had been battered into submission by her blockish frame, now clad in fetching lime green lederhosen that set off her dyed pixie haircut.

"Imogen, what a surprise. What can I do for you?" Bauer welcomed her visitor.

The dean's steel-gray eyes glittered with pleasure. She loved her job, which consisted of ensuring that no student

under any circumstances received the room of his or her choice
and that any parties that might subsequently be hosted in those
rooms were instantly squashed as flat as an armadillo by an
eighteen-wheeler on I-90 west of Laredo. Every day, student
supplicants came into the NoFun office requesting this or that
small favor, and every day the dean got to play a reverse Molly
Bloom.

They asked her with their eyes to ask again *no* and then
they asked would she *no to say no* so they could feel her breasts
iron-clad no and her heart was going like mad and *no* she said
no she wouldn't. No.

DAVID CALBERT

10.

The Morgan-Steinberg Memorial Library at Underhill College hummed with the sound of fingers tapping keyboards, straws sucking up the last precious drops of liquid motivation from Red Bull cans, and freshmen panicking. Grace hated the library, but Imogen had a test coming up and transformed their room into a sea of note cards and Starburst wrappers. The sound of Imogen biting her nails to nubs was a refrain Grace could listen to no more. The likeliest place to finish her own work in peace was the library, even if she no longer cared a fig for the work and only pursued it out of some atavistic sense of responsibility.

The building was a sprawling, spiky behemoth, taking up the better part of a block, which was necessary because it was only two floors high. It had been built during one of those regrettable moments when "modern" meant sheet metal, sharp angles, and sprawl. The floors were carpeted in a burnt orange, and the walls were colored cream. It was a loathsome palette as far as Grace was concerned, but better than drowning in Imogen's mess.

When she entered, a shift worker she recalled from a class the year before saluted her. He was blond and squat, wearing a Che Guevara shirt and a hat with a hammer and sickle on it. Back in class, she had privately nicknamed him Pretentious McFloppyhair. Walking away from him, Grace found a corner with plush chairs and low tables, perfect for resting feet and beverages on. She threw her bag to the ground.

"Shhhh!"

Grace looked around in confusion before her eyes settled on a woman sitting about four feet away from her. She was dressed in flannel pants and an Underhill hoodie and had a quilt draped over her shoulders. She stared at the newcomer with a look of intense anger. Grace pointed at herself in confusion. "I'm sorry," she whispered. "Is this the quiet section? I didn't think I was that—"

"Shhhh!" The woman gritted her teeth before turning back to her computer and typing furiously. On the table next to her was a cup of coffee and a gallon bag of chocolate-covered espresso beans.

"Okay," Grace said to herself and unzipped her bag to pull out her laptop.

"Shhh!"

"Okay!" Grace hissed in return. "I get it. I'm moving. You've won. Celebrate your victory in silence." Grace snatched up her things and stormed away.

She decided she would see if any of the study rooms were free and took a spiraling set of stairs to the second floor. There, the tiny booth-like rooms were lined up at the edge of the stacks. They were private and windowless, nothing but white walls, a cushioned chair, and the knowledge that someone had probably had sex on the desk within the past half hour. The doors were all closed. A bad sign, but she decided she would knock on a few.

The first door opened before she had a chance to knock. Grace jumped, startled, but relaxed as Claire, from her lecture on Medieval Art from a Cubist Perspective, ushered her into the cubicle.

"Grace! Excellent, just who I wanted to see! Come in!"

A layer of beanbags covered the floor, and a thicket of Red Bull cans decorated the desk.

Claire followed Grace's gaze to the energy drinks and laughed. "I've been here for twelve hours," she said by way of explanation. "I have a twenty-page paper due in the morning comparing *Ulysses* and *Watchmen*."

Grace nodded sympathetically, struggling to find a place to stand that wasn't likely to slide out from under her feet. "What's comparable about them?"

"Well," Claire said thoughtfully. "They both took me far longer to read than I thought they would. So there's that. I also haven't finished either of them. So there is also that. They both have male protagonists? And really uncomfortable sex scenes." Claire stared thoughtfully for a moment and threw herself down into her mess of beanbags. "Do you have any Adderall? I've been up for twenty-three hours and I'm beginning to get the caffeine shakes. Adderall doesn't give you the shakes, does it?"

Grace shook her head and edged back to the door. "Sorry." She wasn't certain about the pills, but she was sure that if she did have Adderall she would need it as much as Claire. "I should probably go study."

"Okay!" Claire chirped enthusiastically, pulling her Mac-Book onto her lap. "Maybe I could talk about the—"

Grace closed the door and decided to head to the fiction section. It was bound to be empty.

Amazingly, a hipster with a goatee and long, dirty ponytail occupied the premises. Grace put her bag down as if daring the seat to create another trial for her. The hipster pulled a bag of chipotle chips out of his backpack and began munching on them, letting out a long, appreciative moan.

The chips smelled delicious. Grace realized she was hungry.

He moaned again.

Grace picked up her bag and headed toward the moveable stacks. She would settle there. She could sit, surrounded by books, and finish her damn paper so she could pass this class, pass this grade, and graduate with a degree in procrastination and bullshitting. A freshman was struggling to get the stacks to move by shoving them along on small coasters. Grace rolled her eyes. "You have to press the button," she said to the lamb-faced kid, gesturing to the flashing red light on the side of the bookcase. She moved on, found a well-lit aisle of reference books and decided to claim it as her own. She threw herself onto the orange carpet. It smelled of dictionaries and she liked that. Yes, she thought, this would do nicely.

SURA ANTOLÍN

11.

Clay stepped back from the wall, his brows knit in consternation as he peered at his drawing. A few weeks earlier, his teacher, Allison Tartula, had supplied the class with their latest assignment: bastardize a masterpiece. A girl whose artistic ability Clay had little respect for instantly decided upon Warhol's soup can. Likewise, everyone else was able to come up with an idea by the end of class. Everyone but him.

Professor Tartula had let Clay's failure of inspiration slide and told him to chose a project by the following Monday, but it wasn't until the night before when he had been sitting in Imogen's room, drinking Jameson straight from the bottle and listening to Lana Del Rey on repeat, that he caught a glimpse of the cover of Grace's math textbook. The image there had been modified with nerve endings and bright algebraic symbols he couldn't comprehend, but it was undoubtedly Da Vinci's famous Vitruvian Man, limbs splayed, Roman features cold and unseeing.

When he picked it up off Grace's desk, Imogen had jumped up from her bed.

"What are you doing?"

"Just looking." He told her about the assignment. "This would be cool, don't you think?"

"Sure, whatever, but put it down. Grace really hates it when people touch her stuff."

For some reason the image had clicked with him, and when Clay told Tartula about his choice the teacher nodded slowly and said, "Interesting." He had hoped for a somewhat more enthusiastic response and thought he deserved better than the tomato soup girl, but it didn't matter in the long run. After one sophomore simply added vampire fangs and red irises to a poor rendition of Gilbert Stuart's George Washington, he felt the pressure lessen.

The walls of his self-claimed studio space were covered with drawings and sketches. There were vague studies of the Vitruvian Man on grayish scratch paper and larger charcoal sketches at various stages of completion. In one of them he had recreated the left half of the figure as female. Hanging next to the hermaphrodite was a close-up of the figure's head, drawn cleanly in then garishly highlighted with bright pastels so that it looked like a contestant on *RuPaul's Drag Race*.

But what Clay was working on this evening was different. The drawing before him was taller than he was, and stared back at him with a morbid intensity. The mouth that was normally shut gaped open in a silent scream, the eyes widened with terror. Grace's textbook, he knew, had been for her class with Mr. Davenport, and now the man was dead. Everyone knew he had been murdered, but no one knew how or why, or if they did then they weren't telling. His drawing seemed to cry out in horror at the thought of the atrocity.

"Oooh, very different." Hannah G., his only friend in the class, said as she came up behind him.

"I guess it's rather dark."

"Yeah, but it's good." She pointed her finger at the face frozen in terror. "See? It's so . . . intense. Like, messed-up intense."

"How's yours going?"

"Good, I got Kanye down, but Kim's not so easy." Hannah G. was working on a rendition of *American Gothic*, replacing the farmer and his wife with Kim Kardashian and Kanye West.

"I would have thought it would be the other way around."

"I know, right?" She shrugged. "Did you see what Carly is doing? She's painting a Rembrandt self-portrait with hipster glasses."

"Kill me."

"I'll kill both of you if you don't get back to work." Tartula came around the corner. She had obviously been listening to their conversation, "Hannah G., if Kim's being so difficult then shouldn't you be working on her?"

"I bet that's what Kanye said."

Tartula shooed Hannah G. back to her space then stood with her arms crossed while she contemplated Clay's effort. "This *is* quite a departure from your normal work, Clay."

"Yeah." He scratched the back of his head. "I'm just trying to let it . . . happen."

"As you should. What are you feeling?"

"Excuse me?"

"This image, what emotions are you trying to convey?"

"I don't know. I mean, what with Mr. Davenport's murder and all."

"Who said he was murdered?"

Clay stopped, a bit surprised. "Well, everyone."

Tartula shook her head. "Don't be so quick to believe idle gossip. Davenport's death was unfortunate, certainly, but to say he was murdered . . ."

"Wasn't he?"

"I'm afraid I can't discuss such things."

She walked away quickly before Clay could say anything further.

*

Imogen was in the science building, clipboard in hand. It was late, and she was alone in the second-floor storeroom where she earned a little extra money by monitoring the incoming shipments for each class and sorting them out by teacher. She finished checking off the five boxes of beakers the chemistry professor had ordered and flipped to the next invoice.

It was for her entomology professor, Winston Aberworth. The class had spent the past month studying the behavior of the praying mantis, but a week ago the students had shown up to find Mr. Aberworth frantically running around the room, looking under surfaces and behind shelves. Apparently, all the specimens had disappeared overnight, but then the death of Mr. Davenport occurred and the missing bugs were forgotten in the wake of a murder.

She began sorting through the dozen or so boxes she had yet to look through, inspecting each label. None of them was addressed to Mr. Aberworth. Imogen looked at the list again. There it was, an order for fifty live praying mantises. She went through the packages once again, thoroughly checking the labels of each container before she threw her hands up in despair. Maybe the insects had never arrived? Maybe they had been sent to the wrong building? She didn't know what to think.

*

It was dawn, but Clay had woken at four in the morning. Unable to go back to sleep, he had lain in bed for an hour. Then, when 5:00 a.m. hit, he thought, To hell with it, and went for an impromptu jog. It was chilly out, but birds began to chirp as he ran, and he found himself relishing the peaceful gray solitude. On his way back he passed the art building, and decided he might as well do some work while he was awake at such an ungodly hour. He returned to his room to change first.

Freshly showered and with a cup of coffee in hand, he walked into the studio thirty minutes later. The room was randomly divided by temporary white walls that snaked about the interior like a labyrinth, creating alcoves for the students to work in private.

He stopped with a jolt when he turned the corner to his own work space. Someone had smeared something over his drawings with the same intensity as a child coloring outside the lines. The streaks were violent and jagged, as if executed in a fit of rage. There were areas where the paper had been ripped and clawed at, and a large gash vivisected the Vitruvian Man's torso, so that the paper fell away in jagged tears, exposing the stark white wall behind it. All of his art—ruined.

He peered closely at the smears, trying to comprehend what the strange texture was. It looked like someone had taken a handful of grassy earth and smeared it up and down the drawing, leaving a putrid and textured mess. There were little bits of what looked like shards of green plastic speckled in it.

He plucked one off the drawing and peered at it, and then dropped it with an involuntary shudder as he realized what it was. He may not have been weirdly bug-obsessed like Imogen, but he had seen her praying mantises enough times to know what one of their legs looked like. He looked around in horror as he realized someone had crushed, ground, and smeared insects into his art like paint. He started to back away, but his foot slipped out from under him and he fell to the floor, landing on his butt with a thud.

He groaned and looked down to see what he had slipped on. He was sitting in a pool of red. He stared at it in dumb shock, eyes unblinking. Whose blood was it?

PATRICK PHILLIPS

12.

Carl parked in the campus lot and jogged to the library. He was late. Harsley had sent him a text at around eight that morning: GRACE MONTOYA FOUND DEAD. COME TO LIBRARY. GNS. NOW. What the hell are are GNs? he had thought. Harsley's messages were annoyingly vague. But after he'd computed the news, washed, dressed, grabbed a bagel, and driven to Hurst Green, it was already 8:45. He had a feeling that the detective would not be happy.

The main entrance to the library had been roped off, so Carl had to step over the waist-high caution tape and flash his badge at the two police officers guarding the door.

"Is he still in there?" Carl asked.

One officer nodded. "With the body."

Carl smiled grimly and pushed through the revolving door into the lobby. The front desk looked abandoned, with books needing to be reshelved piled high on the countertop and loose papers and pens cluttered about computer keyboards. Most likely, Harsley had called all the morning shift attendants away for questioning. They were probably in a supply room

somewhere, waiting for a member of the police force to interview them.

Carl crossed the empty study lounge where students normally
sat to do their work, facebook, tumble, tweet, or shop online.
It was strangely quiet, he thought. In college, Carl hadn't had
much time for libraries—there were always too many golf tour-
neys and subsequent parties. If he needed to read, he stayed in
his dorm or went to a friend's. But, from what he did remember,
there was always some amount of white noise in the background.
Now, as Carl walked through the stacks, all he could hear was the
occasional wireless radio beep. Standard police-station sounds—
nothing more.

There was no sign of Harsley. Carl checked the text again,
trying to figure out what GN meant. It sounded familiar. It
wasn't that name of a car company: that was GM. "I'm a detective, damnit!" he muttered. This was supposed to be easy.

Carl came to the end of the stacks and saw a sign that
pointed to a staircase spiraling down like a giant drill bit piercing the earth. The rest of the books must be in the basement.
He sighed and was about to turn around, when something
caught his eye. There was a big letter *F* pasted on the side of the
shelf. Probably some weird Underhill social experiment, Carl
thought. Then it hit him. He was in the F section of the library.
The *G*s and *GN*s were in the basement. Feeling a little proud of
himself, Carl hurried down the staircase.

Harsley and three other police members were squatting by
a stretcher placed in front of several rows of stacks. Most of the
narrow hall was encircled with yellow tape—the scene of the

murder. Carl walked over to them, hoping the detective was in a better mood than usual.

"Took you long enough," Harsley muttered from his position on the floor when he saw his sergeant. "Had a nice night?"

Carl had long stopped wondering how Harsley seemed to know the more intimate details of his life and relationships. Yes, he had had dinner with Kate, but she didn't sleep over. She definitely had not made him late this morning.

Carl let the comment slide. "How did it happen?" he asked.

The detective was quiet for a moment, then sighed and pulled back the white sheet that had been draped over the stretcher. Carl caught a glimpse of dark hair and then the rest of Grace Montoya's face. There was bruising on her cheeks and forehead, and her nose looked broken.

"She was found early this morning by an anonymous female who reported the incident. Probably a student who had a wee too much weed to feel comfortable meeting with police. Strange thing is that another student—Cliff or Clay—reported a bloodbath across campus. It's possible that she was assaulted there but she died here."

Carl frowned. "How do you know?"

"Apparently, one of the circuits in the basement malfunctioned. All the weight sensors in the floor were turned off." Harsley gestured to the stacks behind them. "I've ordered some tests at the lab, to make sure the blood in the studio is the same as the blood here, but I'm guessing that poor little Grace was at the wrong place at the wrong time."

"You mean . . ."

"That she was crushed between the shelves? Yeah, I do. You can shift the stacks back and forth by pressing a button. They'll stop moving if the floor sensors pick up any movement, but, if they were turned off, well, she wouldn't have known what was coming until it hit her."

"Jesus," Carl murmured, looking at Grace's mangled face.

Harsley rubbed his forehead then pulled the sheet down farther. Her shirt had been removed to reveal a heavily bruised torso. It was more than bruised, Carl saw; Grace's chest had caved in, her rib cage pushing toward her heart rather than away from it.

"Grim, isn't it?" Harsley muttered. "Her ribs punctured her lungs, the coroner suspects. But she most likely died from internal bleeding. It was a long death—a painful one."

"She was being punished, then?"

The detective nodded. "That's what I'm thinking. The killer clearly wanted her to suffer. What I'm wondering, though, is how this connects back to Davenport?"

"You think the murders are related?" Carl asked.

"No shit, Sherlock. She finds him dead; we find her body a few days later. Maybe something's going on."

Carl looked at Grace's body again, his eyes resting for a moment on her ashen lips. She had been a pretty girl, he thought. It really was a waste.

Harsley stood up with a groan, stretching out his back. "I'm getting too old for this," he muttered. "I think I'll meet with her roommate and get some background, find out where she was supposed to be last night, her favorite classes and the like. First, though, I've got to call the station and get some backup. We need police patrolling this campus. Two murders in a week— shit's hitting all the fans."

"What else do you want done, sir?"

The detective shrugged. "Find out as much as you can about Grace Montoya. Aren't they close with their advisors here? Get in touch with her teachers. I want to know what was going on with her and Davenport. Call my cell if you uncover anything new."

Carl watched as Harsley slouched off, pausing at the foot of the spiral staircase to light a cigarette. Who had been Grace's advisor? That was easy enough to find out. He stuffed his hands in his pockets and sighed. Grace's body was still uncovered. As Carl bent down to pull the sheet back over her face, he noticed a mark on the girl's neck. At first glance, it looked like an outlying vein, but up close he saw that it was actually a greenish tattoo in the shape of a checkmark. Or was it a *V*?

He thought about calling Harsley for a moment, but decided against it. Instead, Carl made a mental note to ask the coroner about it the next time they met. With a last look at the contorted shape of Grace Montoya's body, he stepped out of the taped-off murder scene and walked up the steps.

*

Forty-five minutes later, Carl found himself in the Art Department, waiting outside Miriam Aarons's office. She had been Grace's advisor for the last two years. Carl didn't mention Grace's murder on the phone because he wanted to see Aarons's reaction. Harsley might be good at picking up on details and reading signs, but Carl was the people person. He knew how to interview suspects, how to appear trust-worthy and caring, because, in actuality, he was. But he was also good at his job, no matter how many times Harsley tried to deny it.

At ten o'clock, Carl knocked on the door. It was decorated with photographs of tropical forests and austere, modern sculp-tures. Before he could examine these further, however, the door swung opened and he was standing face-to-face with a shock-ingly attractive young woman dressed like a middle-aged spin-ster. Carl had imagined that Grace's advisor would be an older woman, but Miriam was in her mid-thirties. She was average height, slender, with a round face. Her light brown hair was pulled back in a smooth ponytail and she wore a cream-colored cardigan around her thin shoulders.

"You're Sergeant Baker?" Miriam Aarons had a soft, cool voice.

Carl nodded. "I am."

"Come in, please."

He entered her office, taking note of the decor. She had quite a few books. The shelves were stuffed and multiple oversize volumes were stacked at the foot of her chair, some bookmarked with purple Post-its. One wall displayed sev-eral woven beige tapestries twisted into geometric shapes. Her desk faced the door and was rather messy. Papers and rolled-up posters covered its surface, and her laptop teetered on top of one of these piles.

Miriam Aarons motioned for Carl to sit down. He settled into a wooden chair facing her, a chair that Grace Montoya had surely sat in many times.

"Would you like something to drink?" she asked after a moment's silence. "I was going to make some coffee. Or would you prefer water?"

"Ms. Aarons," Carl began. "I have some questions to ask you."

She folded her arms, and looked at him hard. "This is about the murder investigation."

It wasn't a question, but he still nodded. "First, however, I have some bad news. You should probably sit down."

Miriam Aarons hesitated for a moment. Clearly, she did not like being told what to do in her own office. Nevertheless, she heeded his advice.

"You know a young woman named Grace Montoya?"

"Yes, she's an advisee of mine."

"I'm very sorry to have to tell you she was found dead this morning."

Carl waited for Miriam's reaction. Her face went a shade paler, and she let out a small gasp. Before he could get a clear read of her expression, however, she buried her face in her hands. His first thought was that she was hiding something—surprise, anger, relief, perhaps—but then he saw her shoulders commence to shake. Miriam Aarons was crying, silently, and she didn't want him to witness her grief. All skepticism vanished from his head, and Carl wished, for a moment, that he could step behind the desk, and comfort her. He realized, with a start, that she reminded him of his sister. Catelyn had been born two minutes before Carl, but he had always felt as though he was the older sibling. Miriam didn't look like Catelyn, but their expressions, complexions, and mannerisms were similar enough that he was disposed to like the woman, even though they had only spoken a few words to each other.

"If there is anything I can get you, Ms. Aarons?"

She held up a hand, silencing him. Before Carl could apologize for interrupting her crying, though, Miriam was wiping her eyes and nose with a tissue.

"Excuse me," she said thickly, drying her cheeks. "It's just I am . . . was very fond of her. Of Grace."

Carl nodded. "I can come back later, if you prefer."

"No," Miriam answered, a slight edge to her voice. "No, I'd rather talk about it now. Please, tell me, how was she killed?"

"I'm afraid I can't say, Ms. Aarons."

"Why not?"

"It's classified. For the investigation. I hope you understand."

Her mouth narrowed. "I'll try." She looked angry, worried, and—was that fear Carl saw in her eyes? He couldn't be sure; she was looking down at her desk now, pointedly avoiding his gaze.

Carl sighed. "You knew Grace quite well, then? I'm sorry, I've got to get the facts."

"Yes." Miriam fingered the cuffs of her sleeves nervously. "She was a good student. We got along well. Sometimes, if there was an exhibit nearby, I would take Grace with me. She was majoring in modern art, which is my field of expertise. Sculpture, although she also planned on minoring in comparative literature. But I was her advisor; I was responsible for her."

"What do you mean 'responsible'?" Carl asked gently.

The professor didn't answer. Instead, she pressed her palms to her eyes and murmured, "I wish there was something more I could have done."

After a moment, Carl cleared his throat and went on. "How long have you been teaching here?"

"Four years. I'm an assistant professor," Miriam explained, without looking at him.

"Did you know Professor Davenport?"

"He was chair of the Math Department. The only time I heard him speak was during the new science center development committee meetings."

"Why were you on the committee if sciences aren't your discipline?"

"The meetings didn't start out that way," Miriam said stiffly. "Ever since I came here, funding for the humanities has been cut. We don't have money for new equipment, new hires. We don't even have enough for the professors currently on staff. Everything's being fed to the sciences. We wanted a recent donation to go toward raising salaries and expanding the Humanities Department, but it looks as though it's all been funneled to a great new science and mathematics center." She gave a noncommittal shrug, but actually met his eyes this time.

"Was Grace involved with meetings at all?" Carl probed.

"She attended one with me. As a student representative for the arts."

"Is that how she came to know Davenport?"

Miriam Aarons shook her head and rubbed her temples. "She needed to fulfill a math requirement, I think. I'm sorry, Sergeant Baker, I have a bit of a headache."

Carl nodded. He could see that the rims of her eyes were red. She had actually been crying. "One last question," he said, "before I go."

The door burst open, and Miriam Aarons jumped slightly in her seat. A woman wearing a sun-yellow blazer and deep magenta skirt stepped into the office. Her auburn hair had streaks of gray and a colorful scarf was looped dramatically around her neck.

"Miriam!" The woman smiled. "I'm glad I caught you in. Have you had time to look over the proposals I sent? No hurry, but I need them by tomorrow."

Miriam rummaged through the pages on her desk. "I did," she mumbled. "They're somewhere here. I'm so scattered today."

"Oh," the woman said, seeming to take notice of Carl for the first time. "Did I interrupt something?"

"No," Miriam answered quickly. "Sergeant Baker, let me introduce you. This is Amanda Pike, the divisional chair of the Humanities Department."

"Pleased to meet you, Sergeant," Amanda Pike said, offering her hand. Carl shook it and was surprised by how firm her grip was.

"I hope the case is going well?"

He nodded, studying the senior professor's face more closely. She had sharp features, and slightly crooked teeth, but, apart from that, Carl thought she was quite attractive. He tried to think of something more to say in response. "Ms. Aarons was just telling me about your problems with the Math Department."

Pike raised her eyebrow. "Really?"

Miriam interjected, "Only that there's been less money donated to the arts recently."

Carl was beginning to wonder if he'd said something wrong, but Amanda Pike just laughed. "That's been going on for years," she explained. "Over half of the professors here used to work in the humanities, but now we've been told to make way for the new. Science, you see, will save the world; the arts are nothing but a waste of time when we could be sweating in a laboratory, finding a cure for all diseases."

"I found the proposals," Miriam Aarons blurted abruptly. She looked quite uncomfortable, Carl noticed, to have the divisional chair in her office.

"Excellent!" Amanda smiled again and took the papers from Miriam's outstretched hand. "Drop by later, will you? We need to catch up."

Miriam promised she would, and with a nod in Carl's direction Amanda Pike walked briskly out of the room, shutting the door behind her.

"What was the last thing you wanted to know?" Miriam had returned to her desk, and was staring at Carl with her clear wide eyes. She looked so drained, so sad, that he didn't have the heart to ask her any more questions. He wasn't even sure what his last one had been.

"No, that's all I need for right now. Thank you for your time, Ms. Aarons."

"Dr. Aarons, please," she said.

Carl felt his face go slightly red. "Dr. Aarons. Sorry."

Miriam shook her head. "It's fine." She extended her hand, and they shook. When she withdrew from his grasp, her cardigan sleeve slipped up her wrist. Carl caught a brief glimpse of green on her pale skin before she turned away, but it didn't register with him. Only when he was halfway to his car, did Carl realize where he had seen the mark before.

Grace Montoya's neck.

He grabbed his cell phone and dialed Harsley's number. The detective picked up on the second ring. "What is it?" he said.

"Sir, I've uncovered something new."

JESSYE HOLMGREN-SIDELL

13.

Alan Connolly had worked in the art building since his first year on campus. He couldn't tell Michelangelo from macaroni art, but that was fine because his job consisted of making sure that students signed in at the door, flirting, and, when there was no one to badger or flirt with, scrolling through tumblr. Two of these tasks were not officially mandated, but Alan liked to think of them as his unofficial duties, especially when he worked shifts that should have been prohibited by the Geneva Convention.

On these early mornings, Alan often enjoyed the privilege of signing in Clay, who was not only attractive and talented and funny but had chosen to sit next to him during the world's longest stats lecture. Since Alan was a twenty-two-year-old man and not a thirteen-year-old girl, he would not describe the tingling that Clay produced in him as butterflies or a crush, but his hands fluttered and tongue fumbled.

Alan was disappointed on this particular morning to find that Clay had already signed in. He looked over the list, determined that there were six students in the studio, and moved to put the clipboard down when he noticed an unfamiliar name. Imogen.

He had never met an Imogen and had not seen her name on any
of the lists before. Unless she had joined a class mid-semester—
unlikely—she was probably a one-off, come to explore the art
building and then vanish. Later, talking to a detective named
Harsley, he would recall that he thought how strange it was that
this Imogen had signed in so responsibly three whole hours
before the studio was unlocked. Then he heard Clay scream.

*

It was cold when Clay was finally allowed to leave the studio.
He had spoken to what he assumed was every member of the
Hurst Green police force, telling the story again and again. He
was exhausted, and his pants were stiff with vomit and spilled
paint and blood. He just wanted to go home, to forget all of this,
and to wait for reality to reassert itself. He figured he would try
to do some homework before succumbing to a Buffy marathon.

"Clay!"

He turned around slowly, half expecting another police
officer, but instead he saw Alan. The athletic young man jogged
toward him, a bag slung over his shoulder and a smaller canvas
bag clutched in his other hand. Clay waited for him to catch up
and tried smiling. He was pretty sure he failed. Alan was nice
in a way that normally made Clay suspicious. Still, it seemed
to suit him.

Alan slowed, and held out the canvas bag, which Clay recognized as his own. He hadn't even realized he had forgotten it,
which was embarrassing. Alan said, "You left this in the studio.

Now that they're letting people back in, I figured I'd return it to you before someone took it."

Clay grasped the bag to his chest and managed a more genuine smile. "Thanks, man. I can't believe I forgot it."

Alan returned his smile, which ought to have made Clay feel more normal but didn't. Clay liked Alan's smile, which listed a little to the left. "Just doing my job."

Clay snorted. Alan's job description ended with dropping a stray bag in the lost and found and they both knew it. "Well, I appreciate this," Clay told him, and started walking. He hoped Alan would take the hint and walk with him. He did.

"No problem. Where you headed?" It was chilly outside, but Alan wasn't wearing a jacket and Clay shivered empathetically.

"I don't know. Somewhere with booze?"

Alan looked appraisingly at him for a moment. There was vomit on Clay's shoes and shirt, and his eyes were red from crying. "Well," Alan said at last, letting Clay steer him in the direction of his dorm room. "Why don't we get you cleaned up, and take it from there. It's Tipsy Tuesday, so there should be something on campus. Probably something at the Will Ho's, or Tyler."

"Tipsy Tuesday? I've never heard of that." Clay was grinning now, really grinning, and it made it easier to forget a disfigured canvas and a pool of blood.

"Oh, yeah," Alan said, laughing. "Mimosa Monday, Tipsy Tuesday, Wasted Wednesday, Thirsty Thursday, Fucked Up Friday, Shwasted Saturday." Despite threats and edicts from the office of the Dean of Norms and Fundamentals, students found a way to partake of multiple legal and illegal substances.

"What about Sunday?"

Alan placed a patronizing hand on Clay's shoulder as Clay unlocked his door and let them inside. "That, young padawan, is your day of rest, because otherwise your liver will rebel."

Clay laughed, leaving Alan in the hall and closing the door. He quickly changed into a relatively clean pair of jeans and a blue-striped button-up. He slipped his feet into clean Vans and put his vomit-stained Converses in the sink with a capful of detergent. He washed his face, brushed his teeth, and stared at himself in the mirror for a few seconds to verify that he looked human.

"Close enough," he muttered, and let Alan drag him off to a party.

The Williams Houses, or Will Ho's, were all connected by strangely angled corridors. Reserved for juniors and seniors, they were loud and drunken and situated nicely off the path of tour groups, so that Underhill's integrity could remain intact. Alan was right. Three of the dorms were having parties, and he led Clay to Will Ho 4, where his friends lived.

Alan banged on the door until a man with scraggly brown dreadlocks opened it. He gave a one-armed hug and ushered them into a common room whose brick walls were covered in rainbow chalk etchings that had the effect of collegiate cave paintings. It was early to be drinking, but a group had gathered with tequila and limes and the dreadlocked man was pulling red Dixie cups and cranberry juice from the fridge and shelves, along with a bottle of vodka that could have been used for drain cleaner.

Feeling suddenly anxious and overwhelmed, Clay turned to Alan. "I've never been to an upper class party before."

"Same as any other party. Go mix yourself a drink and I'll see what can be done about music."

Clay was left alone. He mixed a drink, then another drink. No one was paying attention to him, which was both a good thing and worse than he could have anticipated. He didn't want a crowd of concerned half-friends, but sitting alone in a strange dorm drinking gas station liquor felt infinitely worse. Clay wasn't sure what he had been hoping for by coming to this party, but he was sure this wasn't it.

He hadn't liked Grace that much; he wasn't even mourning Grace. Well, he was, technically. He had known her. He had liked her a little, in retrospect. She wasn't a close friend, but she had always been friendly. Now she was just . . . dead. That was it. No more Grace. Poof. Clay threw back his drink. It was easy to believe there could be no more Clay. That was something that he hadn't seriously considered before: he could die at any moment. His mom could die. His mom could die and be one of those people that no one found until their cats had eaten their face.

Clay decided he would call his mom in the morning. Really, two murders in a week, what was to stop the killer—or, Jesus, killers—from killing him? Maybe Grace's blood was a message for him, a warning. Or maybe he had already been poisoned? What if tomorrow, sitting in his History of Typefaces class, instead of just feeling like he was going to die, he actually keeled over? Call it a life. He took a long gulp.

A dubstep song started blasting on the stereo. Still no sign of Alan in the sea of unfamiliar older faces. That was okay. All Clay had requested was alcohol and Alan had delivered. And if

Clay died, then Clay died. He meandered drunkenly to an arm-chair and resolved to drink more slowly.

Several shots later, Clay staggered toward the bathroom. It was down a half-flight of stairs and a long hallway, but he followed the sounds of retching and waited his turn. The world tilted as he moved, indistinct and muzzy. His ears ached from the loud music and his fingers tingled. The vomiting stopped, and the occupant of the bathroom shouldered his way past Clay. The brief contact of their shoulders made Clay falter and he grabbed at the wall. The hallway rocked like a seesaw.

He pushed on, ignoring the feeling of disorientation and closing the door behind him. The bathroom was surprisingly large, a toilet and sink on one side, an off-white bathtub on the other, with black mold growing on the grout and ledges crowded with organic soaps and shampoos guaranteed cruelty-free. Behind him two blue towels sandwiched a bright orange one. Clay made his way to the sink and fumbled with the taps.

The water was cold on his face. He gazed at the mirror, blearily. He looked like shit. There was a splotch of something disgusting on his ear—possibly vomit—that he hadn't noticed before. "Fuck," he told the empty bathroom, and braced him-self against the cold porcelain. He felt cushioned, like some-thing was padding him, keeping him away from all of the hurt he thought he should be feeling.

There was a knock at the door, but Clay ignored it.

"Hey," Alan greeted him, entering anyway, and smiling like he was trying for Miss Congeniality. "How are you doing?"

Clay thought he might cry.

"Clay?" Alan closed the door behind him and locked it. Clay was suddenly aware how small the bathroom really was. Alan was too close. "Are you okay? Shit, you look terrible. Do you want to leave?"

"I don't get death," Clay said, and prided himself on sounding only half as hysterical as he felt. "Like, it doesn't make any sense to me. I don't get it, I don't."

Alan reached out and tilted Clay's head up. "Is this the part where we have a drunken conversation about life, death, and taxes?"

"Or," Clay suggested, and pressed his mouth to Alan's. Alan's hand moved to cradle Clay's face, and then he was kissing back, engaging Clay's lips and tongue and teeth. He tasted like piña coladas and cigarettes. Alan latched onto his neck, pressing kisses and sucking gently, breathing hotly against his skin.

Clay felt the room tilt again, only this time into focus. He wasn't sober, he knew that, but he was keenly aware of his surroundings. He watched the two of them in the mirror, Alan sucking at his neck like he meant to leave a bruise.

"Can I?" Alan asked, and then his hand was creeping along Clay's jeans to his fly and slowly pulling his zipper down. Clay nodded, watching himself in the mirror, seeing the flush on his face but not feeling it.

"Please," Clay said, and Alan's hand snaked into Clay's boxers. "Please."

Clay's hips moved with Alan's hand, back and forth, as Alan pressed kiss after kiss on his neck and face and lips. Clay thought about his first kiss (seventh grade with his best friend) and his first fuck (sophomore year of high school with a friend who ignored him after that night). He couldn't concentrate on Alan; his life was parading languidly before his eyes, and he didn't know if Grace had seen her life flash before her eyes, and he didn't know who her first kiss had been, but he wondered if Eric had kissed her neck like Alan was kissing his, and if she had felt as numb.

His orgasm happened without warning, rising suddenly and overwhelmingly, and he was sobbing. He realized his eyes had been closed only when he opened them. Alan wiped his hand on the orange towel and smiled self-consciously.

"Hey," Alan whispered, watching Clay with wide, caring eyes. "You okay?"

Clay didn't think he had ever been less okay in his life. He collapsed onto the blue-tiled bathroom floor, sobs clogging his throat and nose, eyes tearing and body quivering. Alan followed him down, wrapping Clay in his arms as Clay bawled. He felt raw, ripped at the seams, sick with the realness of the desecration of Grace's blood and his own painting, the fear of death clawing up his throat and into his mouth with the sharp taste of bile. Someone knocked on the door, but Clay ignored it, crying on the floor of a stranger's bathroom.

Sura Antolín

14.

Marin was neither fat nor skinny, neither tall nor short, and he wore clothes that were nearly as interesting as white paint drying on a white wall. The only unique item in his wardrobe was a plaid button-down shirt with muted colors and small brown buttons. He rarely wore it. On his triannual visit to the barber, Marin never provided a specific description of his preferred haircut. Instead, he mumbled "shorter" and ran his hand over his head.

He was taking three classes this semester: Beginning Economics, Introduction to Spanish, and Library Sciences. It was a light workload, so, out of boredom, he applied for a job as a campus tour guide. Once hired, he learned he was one of only four who'd made the grade.

"Why us?" Shane, his coworker, had asked at their first training meeting. Shane was a tall, sallow boy with a nose ring that could have anchored the Queen Mary. Barbara, the plump woman of minor administrative status in charge of organizing their tours, had swiveled her large eyes at Shane and grinned with a practiced cheeriness that bordered on creepy.

"Well, it's obviously because no one else has as many positive things to say about the school as you do!"

Over the course of the training week, Marin received all manner of tips from Barbara. He was told to wear fake glasses and comb his hair back with gel, to give himself more presence. He practiced walking backward and projecting his voice and memorized the informational blurbs he was to recite about each building. By the end of the week, he had mastered none of them but was nonetheless selected to venture into the field.

"Be sure to wave at your friends as you go along. It will give your tour group the impression of a vibrant social scene," Barbara told him while they waited for his group to meet them in the lobby. Beside them was a plate of chocolate cookies set out for visitors, and Barbara was consuming them as if she had been fasting for three days. Marin fiddled with his fake glasses, which perched uncomfortably on the bridge of his nose.

"I don't have many friends here," he muttered.

"That doesn't matter," she said brightly. "Just smile and wave. I want you to show off our vibrant community spirit!

"And remember, if at *any* point your prospective families seem tired or upset, that's your cue to smile more. You cannot smile enough! When you smile for them, I want you to pretend that you're staring at a basket of kittens. Okay, Marin? Do it like this."

She beamed so widely that Marin could see black clumps of half-chewed dough stuck in her molars. He looked away and wrung his hands.

"You definitely shouldn't fidget, either!" she snapped, still holding her smile. Marin grew more nervous as each moment passed.

Soon enough, a small group of families arrived. Marin couldn't tell who looked more bored, the high schoolers or their parents. There looked to be three students, each with a parent or two, and a few younger siblings dragged along for the experience.

At the front of the pack was a girl dressed in a tube top, a miniskirt, and plastic platform heels, all colored in various shades of neon. She was standing so pigeon-toed that Marin wasn't sure the posture was authentic. She sucked on a milk-colored lollipop with such blatant depravity that Marin felt the urge to gag. Behind her stood a short, pudgy, stunningly greasy-haired guy who seemed at least three years too old to be a prospective student for an undergraduate degree. He looked almost as nervous as Marin felt but was nonetheless staring shamelessly at lollipop girl's butt, a scantily clad but ultimately unremarkable asset that protruded obscenely due to her stance. Marin shared a brief and terrifying moment of eye contact with a huge father-type who squinted menacingly at Marin and thrust his chin out. He had his arm draped around his wife, who seemed about to break into tears at the loss of her darling. Standing beside the huge man was an almost pretty young girl wearing a gigantic pair of black aviator sunglasses, despite Underhill's trademark dim lighting.

Doing as instructed, Marin introduced himself and led them out of Admissions. As they departed, he glanced back into the building and saw his boss staring at him. Wordlessly, Barbara put her fingers to the corners of her mouth and dragged a gigantic smile across her face. Marin forced back the urge to shudder.

*

The tour did not go well. Marin tripped twice, once on a tree root and once on an abandoned volume of Hegel, complete with a Morgan-Steinberg stamp on its cover. He forgot entire sections of absolutely essential information, and watched as the girl with the sunglasses simply walked away. Actually, he thought, she'd probably fit in well. Eleven buildings after he had left Admissions, Marin was focusing solely on how close he was to the end of this gauntlet of shame.

With the group that remained, Marin approached the art building, their final stop. He stepped inside, tripped a third time, and landed in a cold puddle of someone's spilled coffee. Despite himself, he openly cursed, and caught a glimpse of the huge, threatening man shaking his head. The greasy boy laughed audibly. Marin scrambled up and mumbled an apology, racking his brain for what he was supposed to tell them about the Art Department. He drew a blank.

"Does anyone have any questions?" he asked meekly. The group stared back at him, and it wasn't until the awkward trailing silence had grown unbearable that Marin began to shuffle deeper into the building. He planned to walk by the current student work installed in the hallway, where perhaps the art would speak for itself and he wouldn't have to say anything.

"Aren't you going tell us about the Art Department first?" asked the lollipop girl's mother, who was wearing a sun hat so large that people gave her a wide berth for fear of being clipped.

"Well . . . uhh . . . do you have any specific questions?"

"What about class size?"

"Oh, I think it's pretty small."

"You *think*?"

"I'm not an art student."

"But I'm sure they've told you about the class sizes and stuff, right?"

"Uhhh, right . . . yeah, they have, but . . . I can't exactly remember right now."

The woman let out a snort of exasperation.

"Are there private art lessons? My daughter got an award at her high school's art festival, so she'll get some preference within the department, right?" she asked. The lollipop girl winked lewdly.

"Yeah . . . sure, I bet she can get preference." He had no idea whether this was true, but the mom seemed satisfied. They were starting to look tired. He remembered his boss's words and forced a huge smile onto his face.

"Why are you grinning like that?" asked the woman with the large hat, alarmed. Marin dropped the smile and stared at his feet, embarrassed and at a loss for how to respond. Desperately, he looked around and spotted another student walking toward them. The student was tall, wearing a battered, black leather jacket, and had a cigarette stuck behind his pierced ear. He had spiked his hair into a huge mohawk, and his gel gave his hair a purplish gleam. Without thinking, Marin waved enthusiastically.

"Do I know you?" the kid growled. Everyone in the tour group stared at Marin.

"Oh . . . uhhh . . . n-no, you just look like someone I know. . . . Sorry," Marin stammered.

"I look like someone you know?" the punk repeated, incredulously. He didn't wait for an answer and kept walking right past them. Marin heard him mutter, "Fucking weirdo."

He didn't get a chance to regain any composure.

"Do a lot of students use violent language here?" the huge, intimidating father asked.

"Uhh, not really, just him I think."

"How do you know? I thought you didn't know him."

"Yeah, no, people here are very nice to—"

"Why did you even do that?" asked the too-old-for-this-tour boy.

"I—"

"You said there was a deep sense of interconnectedness between students here, but that guy looks like he'd rather get in a fight."

"Yeah, yes, definitely, there's some—"

"There are? I've heard about some violence at this campus."

"No, no, I'm sure—"

"Violence? Are you talking about the murders?"

"Oh, gosh, no, that's entirely—"

"What murders? You mean the professor?"

"Or the student?" added the lollipop girl's mother.

"Yes, but that's something the school is—"

"Does *everybody* get murdered here?" asked the little girl standing in the front. She was holding her mother's hand. Everyone fell silent, waiting for his answer. In silent agony, Marin tried to picture baskets of kittens.

KIT HOWLAND

15.

On Imogen's first day at Underhill, she had paced around her new, undecorated room, anxious to meet her roommate. The first time she laid eyes on Grace, Imogen experienced a rush of nauseous excitement and hand-sweaty lust that would later come to characterize so many of their interactions. Grace wore a sundress for registration, long and cotton with images of sunflowers blossoming down the front. The rest of the freshmen class was clad in jeans and crop tops. Grace ran back to their room and rummaged through her antique trunk, searching, in tears, for something more essentially Underhill. After watching Grace fail to find anything acceptably slouchy and revealing, Imogen offered her the use of her wardrobe and Grace lit up like a cigarette, wiping her tears on Imogen's sweatshirt. Imogen borrowed the sundress and opted to forget to return it. She held it close to her face, breathed Grace in and let the nervous chill of her crush thrum through her body until Grace arrived home.

Detective Harsley made Imogen nervous, too. Not the heart thumping excitement that Grace inspired, but a queasy uneasiness, like she was hiding something. Imogen wasn't hiding anything. Detective Harsley watched her closely, and she noticed herself fidgeting under the thousand-watt bulb of his scrutiny. She commanded her knees to stop bouncing. When she realized she hadn't moved at all in thirty seconds, she decided that rigor mortis was probably more suspicious, and began to fidget again. Imogen had never interacted with the police before, save once when she had asked for directions. She decided she would just have to be honest and charming and hope for the best.

"Do you know why I'm here?" He didn't face her; instead, he studied her desk, Grace's desk, and their collective hodge-podge of trinkets and movie ticket stubs and empty cans of Red Bull and half-full bottles of coconut rum and gin.

"Grace is dead." She squeaked a little when she spoke. Embarrassed, she cleared her throat and wiped at her eyes. She was already failing at charm. When she felt like her voice was under control, she offered, "Clay told me. Sent me a text." At least she could manage honest.

Harsley gave her a once-over and she stiffened. He slumped into the chair by her desk, and Imogen tucked her feet up onto the bed, leaning back into a pile of clean laundry she hadn't gotten around to cramming into the plasticky contraption that Underhill called a dresser. "How are you holding up?" was the first real question he asked her.

"Fine," she replied, and then remembered that she was supposed to be honest. "Actually," Imogen said with a little bit more confidence, "I'm kind of a mess."

"Just do your laundry?" he asked, looking from the pile of indie folk band T-shirts and gray hoodies to the bottle of detergent on the floor, its cap only half screwed on.

"Yeah, I couldn't sleep," she sniffled. "I thought it might be nice to have some clean clothes and that was, like, six this morning." Imogen bit her lip, worried it back and forth between her teeth. She pushed her glasses up her nose. She looked anywhere but at Harsley. "She wasn't here, before you ask. She wasn't here when I woke up. I figured she passed out at someone else's, you know, happens sometimes. She was really torn up about Eric, I'm sure she told you. I figured she was drunk on someone's couch, and I had no clean pants so I did my laundry. . . . How did she die?" Imogen realized she was rambling and tried not to feel embarrassed, but her cheeks flushed, and she noticed Harsley taking note.

He didn't answer her question. "When did you last see Grace?"

"Last night. We had a little . . . fight, I guess? Just a little one. I couldn't stand Eric, you know? Like what he was doing to her was just wrong, and she was so convinced that he was going to leave his wife, and there was just no way. No way." She watched Harsley pick up a frame with a photo of Imogen and Grace, the two of them smiling at some school function—an art show, Imogen thought, but she couldn't quite remember. They looked happy, though. "He was using her. She could have done better."

Harsley darted a look at her, then back to the photo. "I take it your feelings weren't reciprocated?"

Imogen felt her cheeks flushing again. It irritated her that he knew. It irritated her that he had taken one look at her face, streaked with tears and blue mascara, and had instantly inferred that she was the kind of loser who fell in love with her best friend and roommate.

She had just about formed a coherent and scathing response, possibly involving insults about his character, hair, and suit, when Harsley stopped her. "What do you know about Eric Davenport's wife? Nobody else mentioned her." He put the photo down, and stared at Imogen again. She wondered if he thought she was lying.

Imogen rolled her eyes. "Yeah, a former student of his, too, gross. They've been married like two years now. He had that terrible gaudy platinum wedding ring. All the science teachers made fun of it; it's really hideous. I work in the labs, and his twenty-four-year-old wife and that ring are good material for . . . " She paused. "Analytical discussion on the subject of relationships." She smiled weakly. "Please don't tell anyone I told you this, I don't want to lose my job."

Harsley stood, a frown forming on his face. The way she worried about speaking to him made him wonder if she'd spoken to anyone else. So he asked, "Does anyone else know this?"

Imogen's face turned red. "Only the dean."

"That's fine," he reassured her. "And thanks for your time. I'll let you know if I have any more questions. But here's my card in case you remember anything else."

Imogen nodded and tucked the card into her pocket, a little confused, but apparently grateful, as if he'd handed her a twenty-dollar bill.

Harsley was halfway into the hall when he turned back and asked, "Did Grace, to your knowledge, have a tattoo? On her neck?"

Imogen took a moment to picture the graceful arch that she had gazed at longingly—sometimes when Grace was asleep. She would imagine running her hands across it, her lips, the way it would pucker into goose bumps under her kiss. "No," Imogen told him, "I don't think so. But maybe she got it recently? But I said we'd had a little bit of a fight, and she'd been spending so much time with him."

Harsley nodded and said, "Okay then. Stay on campus. We'll let you know if we have more questions," and then he shut the door behind him.

Imogen exhaled in relief and decided to handle her feelings the way she handled her Sexuality Crisis, and her Final Paper Is Due In The Morning Crisis, and her No One Is Going To Love Me If I Work With Bugs Forever Crisis: shots for breakfast. She looked at the alcohol on her desk, and chose the coconut rum as a fruity way to start her day. Well, one shot for breakfast, another to make sure that she that she was really driving the point home, and a third for good luck. The fourth was mostly accidental, because she couldn't quite remember if she had taken the third, and the fifth was entirely on purpose, because at that point one more shot hardly made a difference.

Except, somewhere around the fifth shot, it occurred to her that this was Grace's stash, not her own. Grace wouldn't miss it—really, if there wasn't booze in heaven, Imogen couldn't imagine what was supposed to be so great about the afterlife—but she still felt like she was stealing.

Grace was dead. Imogen curled drunkenly into her pile of laundry and decided she was probably not going to make it to class today.

*

It was evening by the time Harsley left campus. He was exhausted, knees aching with the strain of investigating, head throbbing, and back sore. He wished he had a hot tub, or a big enough bath to cover his steadily expanding gut. Instead, he hauled himself painfully out of his car, into his apartment, and over to the plastic kitchen table—which Lisa had loved—where he poured himself several fingers of bourbon and tried to come to terms with the fact that this case might be beyond him.

It *wasn't* beyond him, though. At least he was pretty sure it wasn't. If he was honest with himself, which was something he tried very hard not to be, Harsley needed a sounding board, and Carl was an idiot. Not a complete idiot; the man had intuitions about people that left Harsley a bit jealous, but he couldn't fire ideas back at Harsley with Lisa's brand of rapid, cold logic. He poured himself another drink and struggled out of his leather shoes, using the opposite foot for leverage.

Lisa's understanding, really, was the crux of his problems. She was an itch at the back of his mind that distracted him from the task at hand, no matter what that task was. Missing her was no more pressing than other thoughts: Carl's incompetence, Kate's breasts, his car's shitty heating system, but it was a part of the never-ending loop of connections and associations that made him such a good detective and kept him frequently on edge.

Lisa understood how he thought, how he spoke, how he worked a case. She had witnessed him at his best, and had been the unintentional audience to his worst. She understood why he had done what he had done, even as she left him, and that had made the Lisa-shaped absence in his life more terrible.

He settled into the living room couch, a plush, green atrocity that he and Lisa bought for their first apartment. He lay back, fished his notebook out of his pocket and dialed her number before he realized what he was doing. It was not the number of their matching cells but the number of her new home that he had memorized and then sworn that he would never use.

"Hello?" She sounded tired.

Harsley regretted the call immediately. He resolved to hang up even as he heard himself say, "Hi, Lisa."

"Is this—? Jesus, what are you doing? Is something wrong?"

"I don't know." That was true. Harsley didn't know what he was doing. He took a swig of his drink. "I have this case. It's kicking my ass, Lis. I don't know what to do."

Lisa didn't say anything, didn't even breathe, and Harsley figured she had hung up. He deserved that. After a moment she sniffled, then sighed. "Okay. Jesus fucking Christ. Okay. Is it . . . Do you . . . Are you asking for my help?"

Harsley considered this. He didn't want to be in her debt because he was still angry—she left him, after all—but the familiarity of her aid was appealing. "Please."

"Richard's going to be home in twenty, so that's as long as you got."

Harsley grunted affirmation and finished off the drink. "I thought his name was Ronnie."

Lisa laughed. She had a nasal laugh, unattractive, but he'd always liked it. "I know you did. Well, what are you waiting for, Detective? Gimme all the gory details."

"Okay," Harsley agreed, and threw his legs onto the couch. "We got this professor, Davenport, who was offed a few days ago, followed by a student of his."

She hummed thoughtfully. "Why aren't you thinking murder-suicide?"

"How do you know I'm not?" Harsley flipped through some pages in his notebook, finding his notes from his conversation with Grace. She had seemed so smart, but so poorly put together. Young, he thought. She had seemed so young.

Lisa laughed again. "You wouldn't have called. So not a murder-suicide, but they were having an affair."

"I never said that," he argued, but she knew him well enough to hear the things he didn't say. "He was married. I'm still trying to catch his widow at home. Apparently, he had this heinous wedding ring, but so far we can't find it. Maybe he wasn't wearing it because he was fucking his student, according to her roommate. Who also has the hots for victim number two."

"Co-ed rooming? How twenty-first century."

"Nope, think more Grecian." Harsley realized he was grinning a dopey, liquored-up grin and tried to stop it, but his face kept the shape to spite him. "Anyway, her roommate was suspiciously where we found some evidence, before that building was even open."

"You think someone's framing her?"

Harsley didn't know. "Maybe. Maybe it *was* a murder-suicide. Maybe someone who doesn't like the roommate is using this as a chance to get back at her. But wait, I haven't told you everything. The girl was found in the library, but there was blood all over an art studio across campus. And then there's this tattoo that the dead girl had, a green check mark. Carl said her advisor has the same."

"She sleeping with the entire faculty?"

He frowned. "Maybe. I don't think so. I have a feeling the tattoo is going to be postmortem." In which case—in which case Harsley had no idea where to look. The townies might know something. He could send Carl to talk to those twin boys again, get a different perspective. Harsley figured he should probably talk to Grace's advisor, too, maybe to Imogen's, just to make sure Carl hadn't missed anything.

"In which case, not a murder-suicide and the roommate is the suspect?"

"Yeah. It'd help if we could find Davenport's wedding ring, figure out who took it—and then there's the bugs! I swear to

God, Lisa, this case is driving me nuts. Praying mantises crushed all over the place, bugs in the guy's stomach, it's sick, and—you guessed it—the roommate plays with bugs. As a major. But I don't think a student could do this." He sighed, his head spinning. There were too many leads.

"Hey," she said after a moment, quiet and tender, sounding like she did when he woke her up by running his fingers through her hair.

"Hey, yourself." He had laid her down on this very couch, kissed her until she shook, touched her until she quaked, I-love-you's on his lips. He had wanted to give her everything. "I'm sorry," he said, because he was, and because it had been too long since he had told her.

"I know."

She had wanted kids. He hadn't. He hated kids; he had seen too many die in too many horrific ways. People were easy enough to kill, but children? Children died at the drop of a hat. She had yelled. He couldn't get his dick up. He thought that he had just lost the urge, that it had left with the images of little blond children with their heads smashed in, but he figured it out after Maxine-from-HR and Myyna-the-flight-attendant and Samantha-from-the-coffee-shop. It was just Lisa. He couldn't get it up for Lisa.

She caught him wrapped around a blond waitress named Summer. She hadn't thrown anything; she hadn't yelled. She looked at him and said, "Okay," before packing her things and driving the hell out of his life. They had since met a couple times, divvied up their stuff. He was angry with her because he wanted her to share the burden. If he could blame her, then it wouldn't be his fault she left. It was, though. Some fundamental part of Harsley resented her and her happiness with her new beau, letting him touch her until she shook and shook.

He understood wanting to kill someone, wanting to poison them, or slash their throat, or shoot them a hundred times. He understood wanting to dash between an unstoppable force and an unmovable object—or two moving bookcases. It was simple. It wasn't quite right, because there was still that pool of blood across campus, but the school would buy it, and the papers would love it, and a picture would be taken of his boss shaking hands with the college president in front of the Underhill College logo.

"Grace killed him," he said after a moment, and cleared his throat. "Murder-suicide. Crime of passion." He didn't believe it for a second, but the evidence could support it. It seemed like everyone involved had been killed. With no one else in danger, who could it hurt?

Lisa paused for a moment. He hoped she wasn't composing herself. "And the bugs?"

"Framed her friend, as a cover-up, so there wasn't enough evidence to point to either of them. Tattoo was just a coincidence. It's simple."

"Yes," Lisa said. "It always is."

*

Carl's phone rang twice before he answered. "Mmm, hello?" he murmured, sleepily. He rubbed his eyes and rolled his shoulders and tried to pretend that he had been awake. From the way Kate chuckled on the other end, he guessed he had done a bad job.

"Hey, Carl, I thought I'd let you know first. I just finished the autopsy on Grace Montoya and I have a few results you might find interesting."

Carl sat up and groped around on his nightstand for a pad of paper. "Lay it on me."

"For starters, Harsley was right; she was crushed between two large, heavy objects. The book stacks would do it."

"Right," Carl sighed. "Anything else?"

"Based on the bruising pattern, that tattoo you caught was definitely inked onto the victim postmortem, which doesn't rule out suicide but definitely complicates the matter. Also, we found something in her stomach."

"Please God, tell me it wasn't a praying mantis," Carl begged, writing notes on the pad in messy shorthand.

"No," Kate told him, "it was a men's ring, platinum, kind of ugly. Any reason that should be there?"

"Davenport's ring, maybe?" Carl heaved a breath and hauled himself to his feet, heading toward the kitchen and his coffee maker. "Okay, thanks for calling, I'll let Harsley know." Maybe, he thought a few minutes later, sweetening his coffee, Harsley would be able to piece this all together.

SURA ANTOLÍN

16.

On one side of the long conference table sat the several deans responsible for the different aspects of Underhill's administration: Security, Admissions, Academics, and NoFun, each nervously thumbing the latest briefs regarding the investigation. Across from them sat a few select members of the school's board of trustees. And at the head of the table loomed a striking middle-aged woman with a mane of jet-black hair bisected by a single lightning bolt of white. She wore all black clothing, rather like Underhill students, except hers was Chanel. She also wore a necklace of glittering black stones. This was President Mara Yaftali.

The president called the meeting to order. "I've asked you all here today so that we may discuss these unfortunate events that have occurred as of late."

"*Unfortunate events*?" Allen Smith, the board chair, after whom several buildings had been named, echoed incredulously. "That's putting it rather mildly, don't you think?" Immediately, battle lines were drawn.

"Would you call them fortunate events, Mr. Smith?"

"I most certainly would not."

She shrugged in response.

Smith persisted. "Do you understand what kind of negative press the school will receive in light of this?"

"Of course. We realize the potential for backlash if this issue is mishandled, but I think that Underhill will manage to stay afloat in these difficult times, and that—"

"Difficult times? You are handling this in a very lackadaisical manner, Ms. Yaftali!" Smith's mustache bristled at the edges. He looked like a walrus.

"We're doing all we can. The police have been running a very thorough investigation, I assure you."

A secretary entered the room noiselessly and placed a cup of steaming tea down in front of Ms. Yaftali.

"Thank you, JaneAnn."

"That's another thing!" Mr. Smith continued irritably. "It certainly doesn't look good to have the police traipsing about the campus! And what extra precautions is security taking? Surely the force could use a little bit of oomph in times like these? Perhaps if the officers were better at their job this never would have happened in the first place."

"Mr. Smith," Johnny Collins, the head of security who had been sitting quietly, interjected. "With all due respect, my men are working at top capacity. I have an extremely competent staff—"

"And I say, with all due respect, Mr. . . . ?"

"Collins."

"Mr. Collins, with all due respect, if your men were as competent as you claim, we would not be in this situation. We should scrap the whole team and start fresh!"

The room broke out in low murmurs, and the president's hand shot up to silence them. "We will not be making any changes to the college's administration in the near future."

There was a moment of tense quiet, the deans' eyes flitting back and forth nervously between Ms. Yaftali and Mr. Smith.

"I think the thing to do is to make a direct, well thought-out statement to the papers," Mr. Smith said finally, as though he were speaking to himself.

"We have already seen to that, Mr. Smith, and you need not worry about it."

"Need not worry?" he muttered incredulously.

"Yes, Frieda Williston has taken care of that." Williston was the head of communications, formerly a poet who had published two sonnets over twelve years and then blinded herself prior to her tenure review.

Williston twitched in the direction of Mr. Smith. "Yes, as you can see I have handled it just fine."

"Now that Eric Davenport is dead, which faculty member is going to head up the completion of the new science center?" he countered.

President Yaftali clacked her nails against the polished table. "We will find someone appropriate when the time comes, Mr. Smith. May I point out, however, that there are far more important things for us to focus on at the moment than science?"

The deans murmured in agreement, eyeing Mr. Smith askance.

Still, Smith forged on. "I am not referring to the importance of academics here at Underhill. This building has been a multimillion dollar project that has required endless hours of dedication just to see it to this stage. To let the project flounder now without some sort of guidance would not only be foolish but extremely damaging."

Yaftali sighed. "Mr. Smith, the matter will be seen to soon, but at the moment nothing can take precedence over the investigation."

"Well! What do you think, Ms. Valdez?" Smith turned to the attractive, olive-skinned woman sitting to his left, who had been quiet the entire meeting. "Surely you must have something to say about this?"

The woman looked up from the brief in front of her as if surprised to find she was not alone in the room. "I will support the president in this matter."

"What if there are more murders? What then?" He addressed the rest of the room, his face reddening.

Yet President Yaftali's coal-dark eyes compelled silence, and the deans bowed their heads. Yaftali replied, "I pray that there won't be."

"Ah, well then, I'm sure that will keep everyone at Underhill perfectly safe," scoffed Mr. Smith as he rose abruptly from his seat. "If that is how you see matters, then I've said my piece." He shut his briefcase and stormed out of the room, the door slamming shut behind him.

Yaftali smiled catlike at her remaining audience. "Well, now that the obstreperous Mr. Smith has left us, why don't we finish hashing out this matter more peacefully and productively?"

PATRICK PHILLIPS

17.

The great green lawn that formed the quad of Underhill College was flooded with the bodies of students. Clusters of carefully shaved and dyed heads dotted the grass like mutant wildflowers. A boy wearing nothing but a shredded pair of jeans, each of the pant legs dyed a different color, juggled three rainbow-colored metal balls as a friend attempted to accompany his movements with the strumming of a ukulele.

Harsley lit his cigarette and stepped around the performance. "Fucking kids," he murmured to himself, looking for a place to sit. Interviewing the students hadn't been paying off. Most seemed to want to impress him, while others went to great lengths to appear aloof, and he no longer had the patience for leads that led in intellectual circles. He hoped to find a place to eavesdrop on several students at once. Their natural conversations had the potential to carry him in a more profitable direction.

He settled onto a low stone wall and flipped through the pages of his notebook to appear occupied. A group of girls nearby unfolded a large Technicolor blanket and collapsed onto it. A brunette with several facial piercings took off her shirt and applied lotion at the edges of her bra, evidently trying to catch some sun between classes. That or the eye of the opposite sex. Harsley peered at her from beneath his lashes, listening for snippets of conversation.

A young girl ruffled the fuzz of her newly shaved head and stretched.

"So, I know it wasn't the healthiest thing, but I ultimately slept with that guy in the library."

"Seriously? Those posts on that anonymous message board are so sketch. Was he any good?"

"Hey, I think there's supposed to be something in the Crimson Room tonight. A band, or a dance or something. Do you want to go?"

"Sorry, I actually have a level of maturity."

"So, I was thinking about doing a project on mysticism and suffering through the lens of seasonal depression, and I might choreograph an interpretive dance. I don't know, do you think that sounds okay?"

"Totally. Last semester, I didn't go to sleep for seventy hours, and then I got my belly button pierced for my narrative psychology class on personal transformations. I wrote about the experience as the metamorphosis of extreme pain and fatigue, and it was cool. Just believe in the process."

Christ, Harsley thought, scribbling aimlessly in the margins of his notebook. The chance of getting anything besides eccentric nonsense out of these kids was growing slimmer by the minute. Across the lawn, a group of students seemed to be sharing a pipe, passing it in a circle as a boy with spiked hair and frosted tips read aloud from a book with a green cover. Another group used the opportunity of warm weather to indulge in a round of day-drinking.

The vaguely familiar form of Clay passed by, his face twisted in frustration as he spoke, his physical gestures erratic. His cheeks were flushed red with either anger or the effort to keep from crying. The boy with him held his hand and appeared to be murmuring to him softly, trying to calm the wild look scratched into the lines of his face. Harsley waited for them to come closer.

"It's just so fucking ridiculous. I don't know why I can't have a meeting with Miriam that doesn't end with her going on a rant about my work and how it's saturated with the intent to glorify the phallic. She says that I need to experiment with the yonic if I'm ever going to grow as an artist. And I don't even know what that means!"

"Vagina-shaped, babe. It means vagina-shaped."

Clay shot his boyfriend a dark look before running his free hand through his hair. "Well, how would you know?" he snapped, wiping at his eyes with paint-stained fingers. "It doesn't even matter. She never picks my work for art features, and our meetings are always so short. When Grace was still alive, her meetings always ran into my time, and they were together, like, five hundred times a week every week. I think she was working on a special project. For Miriam exclusively. And I don't know why she won't give me the chance to do that, too, because I am a good fucking student."

Harsley refocused on his notebook to keep the pair from noticing that they were being watched. Carl had reported that Grace's relationship to her advisor was a close one, but if they were meeting so frequently, and if Grace was in fact doing work for Miriam on the side, that was something to keep in mind.

He remained perched on the wall for half an hour longer, listening for anything else of interest. When a spontaneous game of lawn croquet with tequila shots commenced directly in front of Harsley's post, he tucked away his notebook and set off across campus. He fished for the phone buried in his pocket, and dialed Carl's number.

CAITLIN MURPHY

18.

The praying mantis has legs like snow peas lined with serrated teeth. Its lime body is part butterfly, part vegetable. Hailed as the lobster of the Pterygota kingdom, it has a notorious appetite for sexual cannibalism.

On the morning of Davenport's death, Ben Rowley found one nestled in the crevasse of the torn carpet in his hallway. He hid the insect safely in the empty terrarium that once housed his beloved hedgehog, Octavian, who died two months earlier after getting caught under the radiator. Ben had finally located the spiny mammal after Octavian's steamed carcass began smelling like warm fruit punch. He had never been good with pets. Two of his guinea pigs died from cancer, and when he was four he squashed his hamster in his sleep one night, trying to cuddle it. An insect must be different, tougher, he thought.

Sometimes he would hold her—he thought the mantis must be a fierce female predator that would eat the heads off the males effortlessly. He called her Medusa, but instead of serpents stemming from her head, she had four wings that extended from and contracted back into her canoe-shaped shell.

He didn't know what to feed her. He started first with a few grasshoppers, but her appetite grew. Maybe it had always been strong and he just didn't fulfill her cravings. Ben noticed her beating the glass at night; she scared him more than real women did. He dreamed of green stick limbs encircling him like ropes, holding him down on his bed with no way to escape the antennae offense.

Ben Rowley had 961 cigarette filters in a jar beside his bed. He was on a quest to clean up the campus, one butt at a time. Ben was a member of the school senate, leader of the chess club, and founder of the Ukulele Enthusiasts' Society (although he played mandolin). His wall was plastered with news articles about the murders happening on the campus grounds. Perched on his bed, he peered out the window at the rolling knolls of Underhill. He wished that he had found Grace, that he had seen blood, but his mother told him to keep his thoughts to himself, because his reflections weren't for everyone and sometimes staying quiet is best.

Ben grew up in Manhattan, Montana, on a diet of Wonderbread and anime. He was a spy every year for Halloween, wanting Carmen San Diego's class, James Bond's brawn, and a Jedi warrior's mind. While most kids were mountain biking and playing spin-the-bottle and hot-box in their parents' garage, Ben was in the basement playing *The Price is Right* on his Nintendo 64. He knew the exact price of most supermarket canned goods in the early 2000s and spent time contemplating the Bush-era inflation of corn raised for ethanol production. Ben came to Underhill for the well-rounded liberal arts education.

Medusa crunched the leaves that he put in the terrarium with her dwarfed T. rex-like forearms. She became calmer, almost gentle after he started to feed her mice pups. Even though she had eaten only two of the tiny rodents, he noticed a difference in her temperament. Ben remembered how soft their little bean-pod bodies were before he put them in the tank. Stroking the mice was like rubbing the buds of pussy willows, he thought. Their eyes darted anxiously; he could feel their rapid heartbeat beneath his thumbs. He set them before Medusa one by one, fascinated by her take-no-prisoners advance. Her thread-sized claws poked out from her mouth and began to consume the first mouse, which wriggled helplessly in her grip. Her elongated mouth incisors were dyed red after the incident, leaving her bearded in blood; Ben was convinced that she was smiling.

Out the window he saw Detective Harsley, alone. Ben had been tracking the officer's movements as he would a migratory mammal in heat, careful never to be seen. He had a smaller jam jar beside the larger one that housed the detective's cigarettes—he smoked Camels and lightly chewed on the ends, turning the butts from round to oval.

Now Ben lunged for the plastic cat carrier in his closet. He opened the terrarium and securely grabbed Medusa between his index finger and thumb, delicately tossing her into the cage that he had reinforced with fine metal mesh so she couldn't escape. He had been waiting for this day. Ben threw a piece of black cloth over the carrier and swiftly made his way out of the building.

He walked toward Detective Harsley, growing more nervous with each step. Staring downward and counting his breaths, he crept up behind Harsley. The man must not have been a very good detective, Ben decided, because Harsley remained unconscious of his approach. Uncertain of what to do next, unprepared for Harsley's stiff ignorant posture, Ben lightly grazed his arm. Nothing, not even a flinch of his wrist. Ben's mind was churning, completely unsure of his next move. He was never good with adults. And he was absolutely terrible with authority. Finally, buoyed by a gust of wind, he built up the courage to poke Harsley twice on the shoulder.

"Uh, hi there."

Detective Harsley turned around, face barren of any emotion. "Eh? Oh. Why, hello," he replied with a smirk, mildly entertained by the awkward freckled boy with a half-grown mustache. Ben stared at him, frozen on the spot.

"What's in the box, kid?" Harsley pointed to the obvious animal carrier disguised under a sheet.

"We'll get to that," Ben replied evasively.

"Well, how about we introduce ourselves?"

That seemed more proper. "I'm Ben . . . Rowley, and I wanted to talk to you. I've seen you around campus quite often these days.

"Are you a student here?"

"Oh, yes. I study medieval history, pre-Christian art history, I also take ballet classes." Ben scuffed his shoe on the cobblestones and regarded Harsley's pant cuffs.

Harsley nodded and took a drag of his cigarette, washing it down with a sip of coffee.

"It's a great school," Ben said, like a cheerful tour guide. "So much possibility, and flexibility." He gave a pained smile. "How's the investigation going? I've been doing a bit of probing mys—"

"It's all going well. We'll have this place back to normal in no time."

"How are you so certain?" Ben shot back. "Do you have any leads?"

"Nothing that I can disclose right now," Harsley answered curtly.

"I want to show you something." Ben interjected, and gently set the carrier on the ground. He lifted up the sheet, revealing a sliver of olive.

"What the . . ." Harsley took a drag from his cigarette and bent down. Face to face with the scaled creature, he jerked back. "Where did you get that?"

"I found her in my hallway, digging at the carpet like it was some bush in the forest. They have very interesting mannerisms. She gets moody before feeding time."

Harsley cracked his neck and stepped back, as if to consider.

"I think it has something to do with the murders," Ben said.

"Really, kid? You really fucking think it has something to do with the murders?" He took his frustration out on the last of his cigarette, dragging deeper and deeper. Ben put the cloth over Medusa's carrier again.

"I'm sorry, uh . . . Ben, right? Have you seen any other praying mantises around?"

"No, or I would have collected them. Medusa has quite the luxury home as it is. She can learn to share."

Harsley threw his cigarette down, eyes still on Ben.

"Although I would not want to deal with the aftermath of having a male in there with her," Ben continued.

"Where precisely do you live Ben, in what building?" Harsley looked around at the various stately Tudor buildings that served as Underhill dorms.

"I live in Machiavelli." Ben pointed across the field at a slate-gray structure with white shutters.

"Okay, we're probably going to have to take that little guy away from you."

"It's a her, and her name's Medusa." Ben hugged the carrier to his chest.

Harsley sighed, exhausted. "Okay, but whatever her name is, she's evidence."

Ben gulped. "I thought you might say that, but she's in very good hands with me. You can send your technicians to my room any time. I live in 2B, second floor. Here's a set of my keys and card." Harsley reluctantly took the keys, and card, which were tucked into a Ziploc bag. He looked down at his card, it read:

BEN ROWLEY

INVESTIGATIVE JOURNALIST & PROPRIETOR OF ODDITIES

BenDragonDefender4@hotmail.com

"I look forward to hearing from you. There's a fine art show this afternoon in the multimedia building, five p.m. There will be pizza provided." Ben winked as if imparting confidential information. Then he kneeled to pick up Harsley's squished cigarette butt and walked steadfastly toward Machiavelli House.

Harsley massaged his temples, but the kid's idea wasn't bad. He thought of the book in Davenport's office and the blood in the studio that they still didn't understand. There was as much art at Underhill as there was manure at an agricultural college.

He called Carl, who picked up after six rings as if he'd been hoping to outlast the mechanism. "Hello?"

"Harsley," the detective unnecessarily identified himself. "Cancel your plans for the evening."

"But—"

"Just get your butt over to the school multimedia building at five. And wear your gallery suit."

*

The air smelled of burnt wood, and a shallow layer of fog covered the Underhill grounds as students in oversized jackets and practiced vacant expressions drifted into the arts building. A banner read, "Out of the Void: A Post-Postmodern Multimedia Art Exhibit." The once bare walls now resembled a brand-new jigsaw puzzle, with seemingly disjointed pieces ready to be clicked into place. The show was composed of various paintings, photographs, projected videos, and found objects.

The first item that caught Harsley's eye was a photograph of a trans-woman sporting blue eye shadow and a rigid jaw. Her legs were wide open, and a sirloin steak had been tacked to her crotch. The artist labeled the piece "Pat." Across the room, a panel of extra-large jam jars lined a suspended shelf; each vessel containing a popular plastic figurine from the 1950s immersed in peppery-dill brine. Harsley recognized an Etch-A-Sketch, G.I. Joe, Hot Wheels, Mr. Potato Head, and Barbie with barbed wire tied around her neck. This one was titled "Pickled Plastic Dependency."

Harsley gazed from a distance at a 4 x 6 artwork that was part painting, part video installation. It showed Chinese troops marching through Times Square with blood-smeared toothy smiles, green berets, and rifles in hand. The piece was decorated with more intricacy than a Portuguese Christmas tree. Two monitors on the side looped footage of Americans at war: Korea, Nam, Panama, Iraq, Afghanistan, etc. Carl stood in front of the screens as Harsley approached.

"This is some weird shit," muttered Carl. "When I was in college, we just drank in our dorms and talked about chicks and football or golf, not about the Chinese invasion of America."

"Dorothy's a long ways away from Kansas," Harsley replied as he handed Carl the business card that Ben had given him.

"So where's BenDragonDefender4 at?"

"Oh, he'll be here," Harsley answered. The room was full now, and a cluster of students huddled around the pizza table. Harsley overheard one girl complaining about the lack of vegan pies. A boy by the meat-gina photo tried to act inconspicuous as he poured tequila into his plastic cup. Harsley smiled.

"Welcome!" a voice came over a loudspeaker. "Welcome all!" Conversation dwindled, and the students and faculty and other visitors to the show turned in search of the voice. "Hello," the voice said. It was Miriam Aarons, standing at the top of the spiffy media hall's glass staircase. She wore frail tortoiseshell glasses and piled her hair in a loose bun, exhibiting all of her Connecticut-cardigan glory.

"I'm so glad we have such a turnout this year given the tragic events that have happened recently. We have a superb ensemble of young budding artists on showcase, and I hope every one of you takes your time with each artwork. This exhibit is in memory of the late and very talented Grace Montoya. Grace was my student and an integral part of the Underhill community. Her smile and illuminating disposition will be deeply missed."

The crowd clapped and slowly returned to mingling and perusing the show. Carl moved over to look at some creepy dead baby dolls that hung off a clothing wire supported by wooden pegs while Harsley loitered in the main atrium behind two girls with the same bright red lipstick and bright green dip-dyed hair. Together they examined a white porcelain object that Harsley believed was a toilet. A sign beside the object read "Wisconsin."

"I mean," said the taller of the girls, "it's just *so* pedestrian."

"*So* pedestrian," her friend agreed, and the both of them circled the toilet as if searching for further significance.

"I mean it's just a regular ceramic bowl. He didn't even get an old eighties lodge-style one with a wooden tank."

"Yeah, that would have been neat."

Harsley wondered if this was what Miriam Aarons had been like in her youth, but with more cleavage.

A girl in a leopard-print jacket spoke to a boy sweating in a raccoon coat. "Your discovered art was so much more involved, like I really felt that it garnered so much meaning to me in my own life. I mean, I got it."

Harsley smirked and interjected, "Sorry, which one is yours?"

"That one." The girl in the leopard coat flipped her wrist to the wall behind them.

A small wood plank held a half-full glass of water with horizontal stripes. Harsley squinted at it, felt thirsty for a moment, and pursed his lips. He had never been the gallery-going type. A sign next to the glass read "A Pine Tree." He shook his head in bafflement and turned around to look for Carl somewhere in the ocean of youth.

Carl was on his third pizza slice when Harsley spotted Ben's reflection in a disoriented mirror that had been shaped in shallow vertical waves to reflect different angles of the viewer's face. Harsley tugged on Carl's jacket, leading him over. Ben turned around when he saw their reflection.

"Davenport and then Grace," Ben said confidentially. "Did you know they both swam laps in the pool most mornings. They'd swim right past each other." Ben looked back at the mirror. "Look into the mirror, detectives, what do you see?"

Harsley looked at Carl with tired eyes as he stepped closer to the mirror. "I don't see anything, kid."

"Look closer. Look at the pattern all of the green frames make on the wall over there," Ben insisted. A V pattern stuck to the wall.

"What the—"

"It's been popping up all over the school. I first saw it cut into some of the trees around this very building, but I only really noticed it when I saw it on the back of Amanda Pike's neck."

"You mean the head of the Art Department?"

"She's always around Ms. Aarons," Ben said.

"Yes, yes, I remember her." Carl recalled her dramatic entrance during his interview with Miriam Aarons.

"Well, I thought you should know. Now I trust you're pleased and will let me keep Medusa as a reward."

"You can't keep the mantis," Harsley replied. "I've got to send them all to a biologist to examine and find out why there are so many of them. It's procedure."

Ben blinked to hold back his tears.

"I'll personally try to get Medusa back to you when this is all over," Harsley said with a sigh. "Thank you for your help. Carl will take it from here." He handed Carl the set of keys and swiftly made for the staircase, in pursuit of Amanda Pike.

JACQUI GOODMAN

19.

Candle smoke mixed with the scent of lavender and cheap wine in the meeting room of the Veterans of Foreign Wars Hall in downtown Hurst Green, about half a mile from Underhill. In the center of the room, a large cardboard cutout of Grace sat atop a metal folding table. Blue and gold streamers wrapped around the table legs, remnants from a Boy Scout induction ceremony the night before.

"Do we have to, you know, look at her?" a girl with short blond hair whispered to her friend as they sauntered through the rusty metal doors of the VFW, passing a group of young women in ponchos glaring at everyone who entered. They wore pins that read LAS LATINAS POR LA LIBERTAD! and one held a stack of flyers headlined: "White Man's Battle Call: The Muted Ring of One Latina's Death in a One-Toned Society." Standing next to them in solidarity, a drizzle-eyed poetess waved a FRIENDS OF FIDEL banner. Another group of students discussed the prospect of free alcohol later.

The two girls were wearing all black—not as a symbol of mourning for Grace but as usual. They walked to the refreshments area and filled a plate from the pita and hummus platter.

"No, thank God, I'm pretty sure her face was too gross."

"Before or after death?"

"Milena!" her friend chided.

Clay walked in holding hands with Alan. They giggled nervously at the protestors and kept walking. "Everyone loves a good martyr," Clay whispered in Alan's ear. When they saw the cutout of Grace, their faces grew grim.

"It's such a shame," Clay mumbled.

"Yeah, I just can't believe this happened here. I mean, Underhill of *all* places. It's incredible. In a bad way, but incredible. Unbelievable. I wonder who picked this place . . ."

Imogen walked over. Her mascara was running, and she wiped a blackened tear as it slid down her reddening cheeks. "Hey, guys," she hiccupped.

They mumbled hellos, avoiding her eyes out of embarrassment. Instead, Clay and Alan looked at each other as they wrapped their arms around Imogen. Alan smiled to himself, loving the knowing looks that he and Clay exchanged. Imogen stopped hugging them, but they held her tight. She burst out crying. Finally, they let go.

She sighed. "Thanks guys. I'm sorry I'm . . . I'm . . . yeah. Hey, I'm really happy for the two of you."

They smiled, and she looked up. "Oh God! Not NOW. Please, I don't want to deal with him."

Ben was walking over from the food table carrying a paper plate covered with cigarette butts. He smiled when he saw

Imogen and hopped a little. Luckily, one of the Latinas de Libertad lit up her one-hundred-percent Colombian-grown cigarillo. Ben noticed the smoke and quickly altered his path toward the future butt. Imogen was about to ask what had just happened when a high-pitched wailing noise cut her off.

A short guy with a mustache played the first few notes of "You Raise Me Up" on the bagpipes as if he was wrestling a plaid, plucked turkey. Next to him, a confused-looking girl in a sundress vigorously strummed any chords she could reach on a ukulele. They had come up with the band name Bag O' Smoked Ukulele and were really excited to get their first gig.

After a few songs, they finished their set with a passionate rendition of "Chariots of Fire" and the room filled with awkward silence.

"Should I say something?" Clay whispered to Alan and Imogen.

"I don't know. Isn't that usually for the funeral?" Alan said.

"I don't know."

"Yeah, me neither," he sighed. But the silence inspired Clay, so he cleared his throat and strode to the center of the room in front of Grace's cutout. "Ahem, hi, everybody."

Imogen let out a sob, and Clay stopped to look at her. "We're all, ummm, very saddened by this horrible tragedy." Someone coughed and Clay paused again. "It's so sad that our good friend Grace was stolen AWAY FROM US." Clay's voice suddenly blared as Ben thrust the microphone from the VFW's karaoke machine up to his mouth. Clay accepted it tentatively.

"So, yeah. Don't forget that we're holding a party later tonight at Will Ho 3 called 'Get Shitfaced for Grace' because she . . ." He scratched his chin and patted the top of the cardboard, as if she were there and he was patting her on the shoulder. "She, umm, really did a lot for all of us. She was a great friend and a role model." People snickered. Alan looked at Clay admiringly.

Clay shrugged and turned to walk away, when he remembered something else. "Oh! And, for those of you who don't know, Grace's official memorial service is this Sunday, two p.m. at Lin Fei's House of Cantonese Cuisine. It's the one across the street from Poppy's Pets." He put the microphone down, moving back toward Alan and Imogen. Everyone else in the room looked unsure whether to clap, cry, or launch into a round of "For She Was a Jolly Good Fellow!"

Alan smiled. "Wow, Clay, those were really lovely things you said about Grace."

Clay nodded, proud of himself, and they kissed. Imogen looked at the window, fogged up from the warm bodies filling the room. She watched droplets sliding down the pane and thought morbidly of Grace's cold corpse, annoyed that Clay and Alan were paying more attention to each other than to Grace's death.

She walked over to Ben, who was sitting in a chair counting his cigarette butts. He had arranged them in the shape of a praying mantis. Imogen sat next to him. "That's cute," she said.

"Thanks! I modeled it after my own pet. I'm hoping to get her back from, from . . ." He faltered when Imogen started crying. He looked around the hall, as if for someone to come over to help.

"I'm sorry. She was your roommate. Do you, um, need anything?"

"No, no, I'm sorry. I just . . . you know. You never expect these things to actually happen. I miss her so much."

Ben reached out and patted the side of Imogen's face. Her hair stuck to her tears and mascara. She stopped crying, looking slightly taken aback. Ben smiled, thinking he had comforted her.

"So, Imogen. I was wondering. You know, Get Shitfaced for Grace? Well, I was thinking maybe we could, umm, go there together." Before Imogen could sneer at him for asking her out, a group of Underhill security guards walked through the door in matching blue jackets. They looked like a motorcycle gang.

"Excuse me, everyone!" the chief announced as if he expected representatives of NoFun to be saluted. "We've been tipped off. Someone saw you guys sneaking wine into this place, and the neighbors don't like it. Everybody out." But then he paused, noticing the cardboard cutout and Imogen sobbing in the corner.

Confused, he pulled a walkie-talkie out of the holster that hung at his thigh. The students stood there, plastic glasses in hand, unsure whether to move. After a few moments of murmuring into the walkie-talkie, the chief reholstered it and glanced at his colleagues. Then he motioned with his head and the security detail marched out, leaving the gathered mourners staring at each other. As the buzz of conversation grew louder, security's dirty white van sputtered off toward Underhill College.

ELLIOT GOLDMAN

20.

Her grief wearing off now, Imogen made the rounds of the cafeteria's various food stations. At the salad bar, she found the mesclun mix and looked at it approvingly. Add some baby corn, some chickpeas, and dressing—it could be good. She was midway through the greens, about to fork around to find a hidden chickpea, when she found something else. A large beetle on its back, legs squirming in the air. Imogen held the insect by one leg and carried it outside as other students recoiled. I'll skip the salad, she thought.

Imogen returned to the cafeteria after freeing the beetle, this time to the grill. She could get a burger. Those were okay as long as you covered them in gobs of ketchup or hot sauce. But several months earlier she had been grabbing a burger when Ben Rowley interrupted her: "You know those have a lower than normal fiber content? You'll probably have a hard time in the bathroom if you eat it." She didn't fully believe him, but his words cut her appetite. Is there anything tolerable to eat in this place? she thought in exasperation. If only plain pizza was on the menu. The pizza of the day was topped with green peppers and pineapple. The cooks had a tendency to be too creative. In fact, they once tried "Everything Pizza" slathered with so much sausage, ham, bacon, broccoli, and ricotta that the tomato sauce was barely visible.

The soup was bearable. A bowl of mushy lentils and rock-hard bread would have to do. Three people were waiting in line for the soup, or so it appeared. Imogen realized that the first person was standing with her back to the simmering self-serve pot, chatting with a friend. "Yeah, obesity is the new bulimia."

"Um, excuse me. Excuse me. Excuse me," muttered the second person in line, a mousy girl.

"Could you please move your conversation? We're trying to get some soup!" hollered the third person in line, whose earbuds made her hard of hearing.

The soup-blocker, mortified, put her hands over her mouth and apologized.

Once Imogen finally had her food, she surveyed the room. There was the table of theatre kids still in costume who screamed, "Fabulous!" with every other sentence. Then there were the jocks, who must have been eating the opposite of a celebratory meal. They wore their uniforms with forlornness as they dolefully pushed the over-puréed mashed potatoes and other muscle-building carbs around their plates. Clay was sitting with some people she didn't know very well. She could join them, but then she would have to make a first impression. Should she greet them with a "Hey" or "What's up?" They would ask her the inevitable question: What do you study? Should she say "liberal arts" or "entomology"? But she had only taken one semester of the subject. Clay would definitely bring up that she was Grace's roommate. What if they prodded her to reveal Grace's last moments? Everybody wants to solve a mystery. She found an empty table for two in the corner.

At the neighboring table, she recognized the boy with the mohawk as Sid, who took writing and asked vague questions in political science class. "Goddamnit, another shitty meal!" he declared.

"You think the food sucks, but you've never tried the stuff at the vegan bar," replied a girl with bleached dreads. Imogen recognized her as the head of the Environmental Club who sometimes manned a table outside of the dining hall. She typically offered vegan pumpkin cake that tasted of baking soda along with a pamphlet that asked: "How Would You Like a Cow to Eat You?"

"Why would I go to the vegan bar if I'm not vegan? What's that stuff on your plate?" Sid asked.

"Seitan."

"What's that?"

"It's a high protein meat alternative made from wheat gluten. And it's better than what's on your plate."

Imogen glanced at Sid's plate. It must have been meatloaf, but it looked like a brown toad crouching in an oily pond.

"What are you doing?" the girl asked Sid. He had taken a clean plastic bowl from his tray and was shoving it under his jacket.

"I need it for cereal," he explained.

The girl was horrified. "Haven't you read the signs posted around campus? Too many people steal from the dining room.

If there aren't enough bowls and plates, they'll resort to paper products. Paper!"

"Oh, please. This school has bigger things to worry about."

The reference to Grace's death made Imogen's eyes water.

He continued, "Haven't you heard about the big science building debate? My advisor let me in on the details. And now with Davenport gone, it may not happen."

"The only reason you care is because you're a science student. A new building costs millions. That money could go toward so many other things."

"Like plastic bowls?"

She swatted at him and played with a dreadlock.

"No, really," he insisted. "Have you taken a class in the current science building? It's as rundown as a poor person's house. I hear it has a bug infestation."

"No, you idiot, it doesn't have a bug infestation. Someone just didn't do a good job caging the praying mantises."

Imogen decided she didn't need to hear any more and tuned in to another table, as if changing the station on a car radio.

"Did you see Marne's outfit yesterday?" said a girl sporting a high ponytail and chic capris.

"You mean the see-through polyester blouse and the bright red jeans?" her friend answered. She had bouncy curls and wore a necklace made of cowrie shells.

"Yes, but the worst part was those giant bangles. It would have been okay if they were those smaller and tasteful Indian ones, but these were just offensive! She's calling so much attention to herself. She's trash."

The curly-haired girl rearranged her necklace. "I didn't think they were that big. The see-through blouse was worse."

"True. But, then again, I have a shirt like that. I just know when it's appropriate to wear it. Oh, excuse me." The pony-tailed girl placed a hand on the elbow of a dining hall worker passing by with a pushcart that was heaped with dirty dishes. A paper hat like a tiny sailboat sat atop her hairnet.

"Yes?" the worker said, holding on to her hat.

"Could you grab me a fork? Mine fell on the floor."

The woman balled her right fist as if she was squeezing a stress ball.

"Is something wrong?" The girl tilted her head.

The worker exhaled through her nostrils, pursed her lips, and then transformed them into an insincere smile. "Nothing at all."

"Well then?"

The worker spoke one syllable at a time. "Well-then-I-will-be-right-back-with-a-clean-fork."

"Thank you," the girl said politely to the woman's back as she walked toward the tableware station.

Imogen rested her spoon in the bowl and shook her head slightly. How could the two girls be so shallow? How could they speak of trifles when Grace was dead? Imogen looked down at her own outfit. She was dressed in Underhill sweats. Grace would be appalled. She thought of the dress Grace had lent her. She could not remember if it was still hanging in her closet or if she had returned it. It didn't matter. Grace's parents had yet to pick up their daughter's belongings. Imogen could borrow Grace's clothing all she wanted now, yet she dreaded returning to her dorm. She felt like she was visiting the house of a dead woman, a ghost. A teardrop fell into her bowl of lentil soup.

MADELINE DESSANTI

21.

Michael waited for his parents to go to bed. Ever since he had given Davenport's papers to Detective Harsley, he had stayed up every night, obsessing about the case and how he could solve it. He still felt it was his responsibility to catch Davenport's killer, and, though he wasn't unappreciated at home or school, he desperately wanted to do something that would mark him out as extraordinary. Unfortunately, his mother had been unhappy with Michael's new waywardness and put him on strict bed watch every night now. Without Davenport's papers, he simply sat in the dark, reconstituting the map in his mind and going over the clues he knew.

However, too much time had passed and his investigation wasn't gaining any traction. It was time to pursue the case beyond his bedroom. He waited for a sign that his parents were asleep.

When the low scraping of his father's snores finally reached his ears, Michael swung his legs out of bed. He sat on the edge, resting his head in his hand, building up the fortitude to act. The late hours he kept were exhausting. He looked around, and a small glass figurine glinted in the moonlight. It was a bishop from his chess set standing silent guard in front of a green hardcover book bearing the title *Praying Mantises: A Thorough Look*. He stopped, suddenly recalling a discussion he and Davenport had before his final chess lesson.

"One critical element a chess master needs to consider is the gambit. Now, please, Michael, listen closely, because this is vital." Davenport leaned toward his student, and Michael saw the seriousness in his green eyes.

"Yes, sir." He swallowed.

"The gambit is a chess move in which the player knowingly sacrifices one of his pieces to obtain a more advantageous position." Davenport's voice shook as he continued: "This is imperative not only in chess, but in life." There was a long pause. Davenport's eyes slid past Michael toward the small metal cage propped on a file cabinet. Michael opened his mouth to ask if they were done for the day, but Davenport began to speak again, almost casually. "Do you know why I keep a praying mantis in my office?"

"No, sir," Michael replied.

"I keep that redoubtable insect, buy it food, feed it every day, clean its cage, because it is a near perfect metaphor for chess. Mantises are solitary creatures, you know, just as you are alone for the game of chess. No one can help the praying mantis. No one can help you to avoid checkmate. Survival is as important to the praying mantis as it is to the chess master. Most importantly, just as a chess player must seek to destroy his opponent, praying mantises devour their own kind for the greater good. This is their gambit. No one wants to sacrifice a pawn, or a rook, or, rarely, a queen, but sometimes it needs to be done so that another piece may dash across the board and checkmate the opponent's king. Do you understand?"

Michael nodded vigorously. Davenport, a college math professor, was telling him something momentous, something he might not tell his colleagues or students at the college. Michael smiled now, sitting on his bed and reveling in the fact that he was important enough to be entrusted with such a nugget of wisdom.

Davenport had mentioned the gambit right before his murder, but why then? Why did he care so much about the sacrifice in the first place? Maybe he himself was in check. Everyone knows, if your king is in check you have to move him out of the way. Unless Davenport was sacrificing himself for his king. But who could that be? He *did* give me those papers the week before he died for so-called safekeeping. And didn't he pause before I left, as if he was going to say something more? Why didn't I remember that before? At the time, it felt so world-shaking. Could revelations be covered over so easily?

He needed to be wiser, more attentive, and more daring. He looked around as if someone other than his sleeping brother was there to witness his discovery, and resolve to act.

*

For his part, Simon was sick of his twin brother. Everyone fawned over how smart Michael was. Now the so-called "mathlete" was getting even more attention and sympathy because of that stupid dead professor. Simon sighed, turning over in his bed. Sure enough, Michael was kneeling on the floor, tucking a flashlight inside his backpack. Then, he rose with a weird, abrupt purposefulness and left. The door closed with a click, squeezing out the dim light filtering through the hallway window.

Simon tore the blankets off and stood on the cold floor. Pulling his pants from a pile on the rug and a shirt from his bedpost, he looked around, noticing a bandana on his dresser. He grabbed the blue cloth and tied it behind his neck, covering his nose and mouth so that only his eyes were exposed. A red pocketknife had been concealed underneath it on the dresser. He grabbed it, stuffed it into his jacket pocket, and ran out of the room.

When Michael opened the front door of his house and walked into the cold night air, his mother woke with a start. She listened for a moment then shook her husband, "Hank! Hank! Did you hear that?"

"Hear what? Cathleen, what the hell are you talking about? What time is it?"

"Hank. I think one of the boys left again. Can you check on them?"

"No, Cathy, stop. It was probably nothing. Can we just go back to bed? . . . Or, now that we're up, maybe . . . ?" He dragged his nails lightly up her inner thigh.

"Hank. Please go check on them."

"OKAY! Okay."

Cathleen turned over and closed her eyes. She was exhausted from dealing with her sons. Hank pushed himself out of bed with a grunt and walked into the bathroom.

Downstairs, Simon paused, his hand shaking as he turned the front doorknob. He looked out the window made of wavy glass in the center of the big white door. A wavy Michael walked down the street toward the school. When the toilet flushed upstairs and he could hear his father's footfalls returning to the master bedroom, Simon slipped out the door and closed it behind him.

Simon dove behind the bush next to the door. There was no one to hide from, but his heart was beating loudly and he was starting to feel like James Bond sneaking into an enemy's lair.

From the bush, Simon dashed to a tree trunk in the middle of the yard. Realizing that Michael was soon going to be out of sight, he abandoned his Bondian tactics and started running down the street. His brother turned into the college's entrance, an illuminated UNDERHILL sign on his left, and Simon was about to follow when a group of college kids emerged from the campus coffee shop not far away.

"Going to Jerry's?" a girl in a leather bomber jacket said to a shorter guy in stretch pants.

"I hear all of Jerry's parties are shit ever since that first one was busted by NoFun."

"Man, he's loaded. If my parents had that much money, I'd buy ten bottles of whiskey, too—and a Porsche."

"No wonder Mary hooked up with him."

"Hell, at a party with that much whiskey, *I'd* probably have sex with Jerry."

Simon's eyes widened as he watched the students go by. A tall skinny guy with black boots was wearing a bandana around his neck, and Simon pulled his own down from his nose so that it looked the same. When the students left, he ran as fast as he could to the street he had seen Michael enter. It was dark except for a white metal pole with a blue light on the top. The pole looked like it hadn't been used in years as anything but a convenient surface to hang flyers. One page announcing "COMMANDEER—A JEWISH JOURNEY THROUGH GENDERS" hung next to another with a picture of a bright pink naked female sitting on a gold toilet. It was taped at the top and bottom and its sides flapped in the wind. Underneath the toilet, it read: COME TO THE POST-POSTMODERNIST ART SHOW! REFRESHMENTS WILL BE SERVED! Simon ripped it off and put it in his pocket before moving on.

"Michael?" Simon whispered as he turned the next corner. The light atop the pole cast a blue glow like an old-fashioned black-and-white television. The street felt hemmed in by the brick wall of a dorm on the left and a green hedge to the right. At the end of the wall, a short turnaround sat like a bald spot on top of a small hill.

Simon dragged his hand along the brick face of the dorm as he slowly walked down the street, glancing repeatedly behind him. He wondered what he would do if a college student saw him. He didn't want to have to explain why he was out so late to some twenty-year-old.

In the cul-de-sac he stopped. A rustling reached his ears, and he searched for its source in the dark. The hill tapered to a mechanical hatchway that looked like an air duct. As he started walking toward it, Michael's head popped up over the ledge.

"Fuck, Mick! What are you doing? You almost made me shit my pants!"

"Get down here! Someone's going to see you!"

Simon clambered into a small air well that led to a wrought-iron door wedged into the hillside. Michael was standing on a metal crossbar in the door, the extra height allowing him to peer over the edge, but he jumped down when Simon entered the small space. College students had clearly used the secluded area as a make out-smoke-drink-graffiti spot. A red beer can lay in a pile of leaves and cigarette butts, and "Allen Ginsburg runz this shiz" was spray-painted on one of the walls along with a Sharpied spelling correction and the editorial comment, "contrived."

"Why the hell did you follow me?" Michael punched his brother in the arm.

"I'm not going to let you get away with all of this after you busted me for breaking the garage window. You're trying to solve Davenport's murder, aren't you? Always wanting to be the hero. Plus, what if you actually succeed?"

"What are you talk—"

"Come *on*, Mick! You get everything. Can't you include me? We used to talk all the time, and now you won't even tell me what this whole Davenport thing is about."

"Calm down, okay? Someone is going to hear us. You want in on catching Davenport's killer? Fine, but you're not stealing the credit from me, no matter who finds the final clue. Deal?"

"Deal."

"Then listen to this. Davenport told me something before he died, and I think he sacrificed himself for something or something."

"'Something or something?"

"Well, I haven't figured out that part yet, but there's this move in chess called a gambit, where you sacrifice one of your pieces to help you win. He brought it up the last day we talked, and it seemed like he was worried."

"Where the hell are we?"

"Davenport gave me some pages of a notebook before he died, and I figured out that one of them was a map of tunnels underneath the college. I explored them one night, but I had to get home, and then I had to give the pages to the detective. When I checked, this was the only entrance that's not blocked off."

"Why not?"

"It's not actually on the map. In the middle of one of the tunnels a sign said e4, one the most commonly used openings in chess. So I figured it was a good place to start. I went there and found the tunnel that led here." Michael pointed to the metal door.

They couldn't see anything through the gaps but the dark unknown of the tunnel. By the black handle was a small key-hole, and Simon traced it with his finger. "He didn't give you a key, did he?"

"No."

"That sucks."

"Yeah."

"Are you sure about all of this? I don't know. It sounds like crap."

"No, Simon. I promise. This isn't just another one of my ideas. I swear to God."

Simon clenched and unclenched his fists, finally conceding. "Fine. Fine, you're telling the truth, but I still don't understand. Was he crazy?"

"Who? Davenport? Of course not. He was a college professor!"

"Well, yeah, but sacrifice? That's crazy if you ask me."

"No. He never seemed crazy and . . . did you hear that?"

"Hear wha—?"

Michael clapped his hand over Simon's mouth, then looked at him meaningfully and motioned with his head to follow. They inched out of the small clearing and hid behind some thick bushes. Simon's hand flew to his pocket. The red pocketknife felt heavy. He squeezed it, tracing the smooth rounded top with his finger.

"My backpack!" Michael gasped, but it was too late. Evidence of his presence was propped against the metal door in full view of the two people walking down the street. Black hoodies covered their faces, and the twins couldn't tell how old they were. They were conversing quietly in the blue-lit dead end. Suddenly, the one on the left slowed and reached into his breast pocket. Michael and Simon let out a small gasp as the shape of a black gun emerged. The twins locked eyes, sharing identical looks of fear.

"What do we do?" Michael whispered. Simon brought a shaking finger to his lips. The two people in black were now holding Michael's backpack, and the one carrying the gun fixed his eyes on the bush.

"Maybe it's that kid who keeps messing around out here." The keeper of the gun started walking forward, weapon pointing at the exact spot where the twins were hiding. The boys looked at each other. Michael pointed his thumb at his chest and Simon shook his head, eyes flashing back and forth between his brother and the barrel of the gun.

"Hey, whoever's in the bush. Out. Now."

Simon motioned with his head to run, and Michael shook his head quickly in disagreement. They paused, looking questioningly at each other, then nodded in mutual understanding. Simon bounced his fist on the palm of his hand, throwing out two fingers at the same time that Michael did. *Scissors ties scissors*. They played another round, and both threw out a fist. *Rock ties rock*. Another round, and finally one twin covered his brother's identical fist with the palm of his hand. *Paper beats rock*. They nodded again, and one of them crawled out.

Together, the two thugs grabbed the boy's arms and twisted them behind his back.

"Hey, watch it!"

"Shut up," the boy's captor barked.

"What have I done? Leave me alone."

Pushing the twin ahead, they walked to the metal door. One of them brought out a small silvery key and slid it into the weathered keyhole. When he did, the door opened smoothly and silently. A second later, it closed with a crunch. The other twin watched from the bushes as his brother was dragged into the dark mouth of the tunnel.

ELLIOT GOLDMAN

22.

Kate dragged a heavy arm out from under her neck to switch on the table lamp and picked up the phone. "Hello?"

"Kate, it's Harsley."

She rubbed her eyes. "Again? You're waking me up in the middle of the night, *again?* You do know that there are twenty-three other hours in the day?"

"Yeah, but this is my favorite."

"Well, I'm not cutting open any more bodies at any hour." She blearily grabbed her watch from the bedside table.

"Calm down, Steelford. I'm not going to make you tong any praying mantises dipped in stomach acid for a second time. I just got home from a student shindig and trying to track down that Pike woman with no luck, and found a message that we have a meeting tomorrow at Underhill with the president of the college. I'll see you at nine a.m. sharp."

"Why do I have to be there? I just deal with the bodies, remember?"

"Look, I'm not sure what the details are, but all the members of the team are expected to be there."

"I'm sorry. I can't make it tomorrow morning."

"Nice try, Steelford. I'll see you at nine a.m. Goodbye."

                                   *

The next morning Harsley, Carl, and Kate ascended the noble marble staircase in the lobby of the oldest building on campus. The stairwell's acoustics echoed their footfall, and Harsley imagined someone waiting for them at the top. Instead, they arrived at a landing and had to make the decision to turn left or right along a wide and empty hall. Harsley led his team to the left. They passed numerous deans' offices. A student's voice could be heard through a thick wooden door: "I *know* the deadline for add/drop has passed, but I really don't think I'm in the right spiritual place to be in this class."

Kate yawned. "Maybe we should have turned right."

Harsley ignored her and continued walking down the passageway. He reached a dead end and turned around. "You been here before?"

"No. Just a gut feeling."

At the other end of the hall, an unmarked door led to an anteroom with two desks. At one of them an older secretary with sky-blue hair sat typing, her fingers moving as fast as a hummingbird. At the other, a younger secretary gazed idly at a copy of *People*. Harsley approached the latter. "Hello. We have—"

She pointed to the typist.

Harsley shrugged and approached the first desk. "Hello. We have—"

She pointed to a door between the two desks. "Talk to Frank."

So the group trooped through the door into another anteroom, where a guard the size of a small SUV stood as if cemented in place. He clasped his hands together and wore a baggy windbreaker with "FRANK" stitched on the chest.

"Hello, we have a meeting with Mara Yaftali," Harsley said. He motioned toward the door, but the guard didn't budge. "Ahem."

Finally, their presence was acknowledged. "Identification, please."

Harsley gave the guard a look of surprise, then turned to Carl. "I think we've got a cop-wannabe." He slowly retrieved his badge from his pocket without taking his eyes off the guard. Likewise, Kate and Carl patted their pockets for their own IDs. The guard read each name aloud and then looked into the visitor's eyes as if committing the face to memory. At last he moved aside. Harsley turned the old brass knob and led the group into the office of the President of Underhill College.

The office was slightly smaller than a first-class suite on the *Titanic* and nearly as elegant. It had an enormous teak desk, several brocade couches and chairs, and side tables that made it look like a hotel lounge. On the paneled walls were interspersed Piranesi's etchings of the prisons of Rome. The president had once been a Classics scholar.

Behind the great desk, buttoned from her hips to her chin in a black silk blazer, sat Mara Yaftali. She was speaking to a woman sitting on one of the couches. The woman had brilliant green eyes and long, ruler-straight jet-black hair. Immediately, she brought her conversation to a conclusion. "It's been nice talking to you, Mara," she said, getting up.

President Yaftali acknowledged her visitors. "Mr. Harsley, you're quite early. This is Ms. Eva Louisa Valdez, of Valdez Pharmaceuticals. She's a very dear friend of the college."

They exchanged half-hearted greetings, and Eva Louisa Valdez left the office. The team watched her pass two tables, one for a single-serve coffee maker, the other for sugar and stirrers.

"Well, take your seats." Yaftali pointed to the chairs. "Good morning, Kate," she said with a new kindness. Harsley's right eyebrow went up upon hearing the president refer to his colleague by her first name.

"I suppose we should begin," Yaftali declared. "Thank you all for coming here today. I appreciate all the work you have done for us here at Underhill. The deaths of our *beloved* faculty member Eric Davenport and student Grace Montoya have saddened the whole community. Moreover, the regrettable events have had negative effects on many aspects of college life. Several of our students have been so traumatized that they have informed their advisors of plans to transfer next semester. Other students have chosen to take leaves of absence. This severely impacts our financial status. And not only have our current students been affected, so have our prospective students. I head a story that one prospective student on a tour asked a guide if all the students at Underhill get murdered. Another time—"

"I'm sorry that the school's reputation has been hurt, but what can we do about it?" Harsley interjected, "We're just here to solve the crime."

"Mr. Harsley, please allow me to continue. No man should interrupt a woman when she's talking."

Harsley coughed to cover a chuckle. The woman in front of him was the president of a college, not a country.

Yaftali squirmed in her chair. "What was I going to say? Oh, yes, with detectives constantly present on our campus—examining evidence, questioning students—the community cannot avoid memories of our recent tragedies."

"So you want us to solve a case without access to the crime scene? You want us to stop collecting evidence, and stop talking to suspects and associates of the deceased?" Carl asked.

"I'm saying you need not solve the case at all," the president corrected him. "You've had your chance. It's not fair to the college—the ongoing bad press. And it's no secret that the professor and the girl had an affair. Ms. Steelford, isn't it true that Ms. Montoya's death could have been accidental? She could have been unaccustomed to the technology of the moving bookshelves. And Eric Davenport, well, he—"

"What about him?" Kate said impatiently.

"Natural causes. A heart attack maybe," Yaftali responded.

"Sorry to disappoint, but the tox screens came back. The man was poisoned!"

"Oh, tsk, then it was a suicide."

"I won't falsify death certificates, if that's what you're suggesting. I'm convinced those deaths were due to foul play. You're asking me to do something immoral and illegal, and I won't do it!"

Yaftali pulled her chair in closer to her desk and leaned forward. "Our college is heading toward a dead end. The school already has an anemic endowment. We can't afford to lose money from a lowered enrollment. In addition, our biggest donor has threatened to cease her generous gifts if the school continues to receive such negative publicity. Maybe you've heard we're planning a new science center. Without the support of the donor, we can't even afford to break ground. I am sure that you are aware that such construction will provide jobs for local contractors. At Underhill, we always try to partner with the greater community."

Harsley stood up and declared, "Screw your science building! We're not going to put justice on hold for a damn laboratory! What about the families of the victims? Don't they mean anything to you?"

Yaftali's eyes widened. "Yes, we all want closure, but aimlessly prolonging this case is not going to get it. I believe we've covered all the issues! Meeting adjourned." She took some deep breaths and appeared more relaxed. "Kate, are we still on for lunch this afternoon?"

Kate looked down at her nails. She mumbled, "Sure."

"Good," Yaftali said with a smile, "Ms. Valdez and I will see you then."

*

That night when he returned home, as Harsley lay on his bed clad in his jacket and tie, he was still stewing over the meeting with that arrogant president and the unproductive day that followed. After a while, he imagined what Grace and Davenport's relationship was like. They probably fought a lot. They probably thought they owned the world. And Grace Montoya's demeanor that day Davenport died . . . she seemed so unaffected by it.

He was tired of ruminating. He was tired of the case. He picked up his phone to dial Carl. "Awake?" Harsley said, loosening the tie from his neck.

"Yes, sir?" Carl answered.

"Listen, there's no way in hell this case is gonna be closed the way Yaftali wants it to be, but I've been thinking she's right about one thing. It's overdue in being solved."

"I know, sir, but we are getting closer. We have more clues. We still have to examine those tunnels."

"I already did."

"What? When? I mean, really?" Carl was starting to sound like a student.

"Yeah, one night when sleep and I weren't getting along. Anyway, I found nothing. That kid probably read too many Dan Brown novels."

"And how do we explain the praying mantises? And what about the V shape those frames formed at the art show? The V-shaped tattoo on Grace Montoya's neck? And the one on that art history professor's arm?"

"Carl, if you don't shut up, I'll call the captain and tell him I need a new partner. Anyway all those 'clues' are distractions. I know the answer to this case."

"You do?"

"Yes. This case will be closed, damnit." Harsley slammed the phone on its receiver, then looked down at his body and

realized he hadn't undressed for bed. He grunted, swung his
legs to the edge of the mattress, and exhaled deeply, pausing
before walking over to the mirror and unbuttoning his white
Oxford shirt. What he saw was wiry chest hair and undefined
pectoral muscles. He threw the shirt to the ground. He desper-
ately wanted to slip into bed, because in fact he had no idea
how the pieces of the case fit together. Maybe he'd dream a
solution.

He unbuckled his belt and let his pants drop. Standing in
his boxer shorts, he scrutinized how much he had let himself
go. Plus the circles under his eyes had been darkening for
some time. His left ear looked higher than his right; the image
in the mirror revealed his gross aesthetic asymmetry. How
strange mirrors are, he thought. The left eye's the right, the
right's the left. And if you try to read something in a mirror,
good luck. He rubbed the stubble on his chin, and his eyes
widened. Unless . . . it's backward.

Harsley snatched his shirt and pants off the floor. He didn't
bother buttoning his shirt, didn't zip his fly, or buckle his belt.
Plucking his keys off the table in the foyer, he flew out the door.

At the station, Harsley opened the evidence bag that held
the strange little book he had found locked in Davenport's desk.
Harsley rushed with it to the nearest bathroom. He opened the
book to one of the pages with the illegible writing and held it
up to the mirror. He caught a phrase in messy script, then more
words became decipherable. The writing was in the format of
a letter.

He looked closer into the mirror and read the closing saluta-
tion of the letter. "Love, Eva Louisa." Harsley's cell phone rang.

"Hello!" Harsley crowed.

"Harsley, it's Kate."

"Kate! Listen—"

"No, you listen for a quarter of a second. We've gotten the
report back about the blood in the art studio. It was not Grace
Montoya's."

"What?"

"In fact, it's not human. The stuff is pig's blood. Direct
from the slaughterhouse. The kid who had the work space next
to Clay was apparently working on a project that symbolized
commodity capitalism and the quest for—"

"Never mind."

"Right, but there's more news. I've reexamined the bodies,
and I have substantial proof to mark Davenport's manner of
death as suicide and Montoya's manner of death as accidental."

"What!?"

"I said I've reexamined the bodies and—"

"I heard what you said! I just don't know what the hell you
mean."

"I found poison on his fingers. It must have spilled while he
was handling the toxin."

"No, no, no, no! What's gotten into you? This morning
you're all 'I'm not going to put a false cause of death on the
death certificates,' and, now that you've had lunch with Yaftali
and that donor you're calling the deaths suicide and accident?

You know those were both homicides! You know it!" he nearly screamed, although he had come close to reaching the exact same conclusion an hour earlier.

"Harsley, can you stop being a detective for one moment?"

"You tell me what went on at that lunch. You tell me what they said to you. Did they blackmail you? Or are you sleeping with one of them in addition to Carl?"

"Good night, Harsley."

MADELINE DESSANTI

23.

Harsley spent the rest of the night driving around and drinking gas station coffee. When he stumbled out the door of the police station, wired and angry, the plan had been to head straight to Kate's apartment. He expected that his sudden appearance at her door would double the agitation typical of their spontaneous late night phone calls, and the idea almost pleased him. He wondered, for a moment, if she would open the door in nothing but a bathrobe, and if it would conform to her body in the way that he liked. Her skin often flushed when she was angry, and the reddish hue accentuated the curves of her breasts. He forced the thought from his mind. He refused to be softened by someone who had betrayed the case by siding with the president of that college. Even if she did have great tits.

In the time it took for the engine of his car to sputter to life, Harsley's head cleared enough to realize that showing up at Kate Steelford's apartment in the dead of night was not the best idea. Given Kate's sudden inexplicable support of Yaftali's agenda, and the undeniable fact that he was drowning in leads, he had to play this carefully. Everything had become a game of strategy, and he could afford no missteps.

He listened to the hum of the tires against the asphalt as he drove, his mind lulled by the rhythmic clunking of something broken somewhere inside the engine. Yet even that, a sound that he had spent the last six months assessing, was a necessary part of the routine. It helped him think.

Undoubtedly, Kate had to be distanced from the case. Carl too. The officer's relationship with the ME posed too much of a risk.

He stopped at a red light and used the delay to consider the suspects and the possibilities. He started with the mantises. They had been appearing everywhere. A statement, one could say. The students at Underhill seemed to be defined by statements; the art show had proven that. An aggressive honk from a car behind him broke his reverie, and Harsley realized the light had changed. He removed a pack of cigarettes from his pocket, selected one, lit it, and took a long drag before moving his foot to the gas pedal. The flash of a finger appeared in his rear view mirror.

That Imogen girl. Strange as it was that she dedicated her life to those bizarre insects, she didn't seem like the type that would, or could, kill. Harsley had known his share of murderers. They lacked the sense of warm humanity that Imogen possessed. And the way she had clutched the card with Harsley's phone number after the interview made it seem as if she was grateful. She would never have the stomach to take a life, and even if she did, the deaths of Davenport and Grace couldn't be her doing. Both were episodes of twisted showmanship, not raw passion.

"Someone tattooed a dead girl, for fuck's sake," Harsley muttered to himself, flicking a less-than-half-smoked cigarette out the window. No, someone who would introduce a praying mantis into the stomach of a professor, who would crush a girl between bookcases and then tattoo her corpse, had an artistic touch. The roommate, eerie as she might be, was out.

The sky was beginning to change with the dawn, color bleeding back into the horizon. Harsley wasn't sure how long he had been driving. He looked at the clock on his dashboard and rubbed his eyes with the thumb and forefinger of his left hand. It was almost six in the morning. He scanned the streets, searching for another place to buy coffee. This was obviously a wealthy neighborhood. The houses were lined with spiked fences painted bone white. Likely the product of a communal housing contract, the buildings rose from the manicured grass like hunkering monsters saturated with the kind of wealth and privilege he associated with Underhill students. In fact, Harsley noted, he wasn't far from the campus.

He pulled into a Starbucks down the street from the VFW Hall, took a moment to buckle his belt and zip his pants, and went inside carrying his notebook. Half-consciously, Harsley registered disappointment that the only baristas working the early shift were male. He took his coffee black, and took a seat at one of the tables in the rear of the room, where he pored over the notes he had made about the people he had encountered and interviewed in the case, looking for someone who fit the right profile. Toward the front of the room, a bell rang, announcing the entrance of a tall, slender redhead. He watched her slide her coffee into a cardboard sleeve and adjust the computer bag on her shoulder before moving to the back of the room. So she was a professional, though not in any particular hurry to get to work. He wondered if she was the type to wake early to get a jump on the day ahead. Or if she was escaping a bad home life.

"Hello." Harsley looked up at her pointedly, raking his eyes across her body before giving a slight smile, kicking the chair across from him out from under the table with his foot. The redhead's face contorted slightly.

"Sorry," she replied with a forced smile. Then she held up her left hand. "I'm married." Harsley shrugged and watched her walk to another table before returning to his notes. It was a shame about married women and their attachments to their rings. In the end, the sentiment hadn't stopped Lisa. Or himself. Or Davenport, for that matter, but he had a taste for students, who likely found an affair's risk exotic. Perhaps it was a status symbol of some kind. Rings. Davenport's ring. Notoriously hideous, with its mate somewhere in the world, entirely unchecked.

"Goddamn it," Harsley muttered in disgust, throwing back a large swig of his coffee before looking for Davenport's address in his notes. "How could I have missed that?" He found the address and cursed his own stupidity. Davenport's wife. He hadn't spoken to Davenport's goddamn wife. That woman had slipped his mind after the failure of his initial attempt to question her. He grabbed his coffee and felt for the keys in his pocket before rushing out of the door, leaving the redhead perplexed but thankful to be alone.

*

Davenport's home was, not surprisingly, nearby. The alien loneliness of the early morning, coupled with the tomb-like mass of the house's façade, gave the grounds an uncomfortable sense of irony or the macabre. Self-consciously, Harsley readjusted his clothes before approaching the door.

He rang the bell and waited, using the moment to remove a cigarette from his pocket and roll it between two fingers. He heard faint barking before the door opened with a slow creak, revealing a tall blond in a silk bathrobe. Pale, loose curls framed the soft features of her face, and the blue of the robe accentuated the deep brown of her eyes. Davenport certainly knew how to pick them, Harsley thought appreciatively, working to keep his mind from his lower half. She brought a cigarette to her lips, slouching against the door frame before taking a drag. Her awful wedding ring glinted slightly in the early morning sun.

"Can I help you?" she exhaled, and a steady stream of smoke followed. Harsley noticed that a ring of pink lipstick had stained the paper of the cigarette, and wondered why she would bother applying makeup this early in the morning while neglecting to dress. He took the opportunity as an invitation to light his own cigarette.

"Detective Harsley, Mrs. Davenport. I'm investigating your husband's death. My partner and I tried to get in touch with you earlier, but you were away."

She sighed and moved to let him in. "I was wondering when the cops would show up. You might as well come in."

He followed her through the small foyer and into the living room, noticing that nearly every corner was overflowing with dying flowers. Tokens of sympathy for her loss. But given the haphazard way they were arranged, it didn't appear as if Mrs. Davenport was beside herself with grief. Not publicly or privately.

"It's Ophelia, by the way," she remarked offhandedly, settling onto one of the floral patterned couches in the living room. She tapped the end of her cigarette into a glass ashtray on the coffee table before looking up at Harsley from beneath her lashes. "I'm not a wife anymore, and I'm too young to be a widow. So Ophelia. Please."

He looked at her carefully before seating himself in a well-padded armchair. "Strange name," he stated simply, watching as she reclined into the cushions, the robe playing off of her curves in a way Harsley did his best to ignore.

"I changed it when I started college. Legally, it's Heather, but that never felt right to me, and I figured that if I was going to use Underhill to reinvent myself, I might as well commit to it."

"You were a student?" Harsley raised an eyebrow for her.

"It was a very long time ago," she said offhandedly, waving her hand as if to dismiss the topic entirely. The look of skepticism on Harsley's face deepened, and Ophelia sighed. "Being married to Eric made all time seem like a long time. He used to joke that I was setting myself up for a tragic end, picking a name like that. Well. Look who's laughing now." She smirked slightly before taking a light pull on her cigarette. "What is it that you want to know about my late husband?"

"Were you aware, Ophelia, that your husband was having an affair with one of his students? Ms. Grace Montoya?"

"Yes. You know, for someone who was obsessed with chess and strategy, Eric was incredibly stupid to think that I wouldn't be playing my own game. You can't succeed if you're counting on the obliviousness of your opponent. Yes, I knew. And even if I hadn't figured it out for myself, a friend confirmed it for me."

This was going swimmingly. After ten minutes, the widow had just admitted a motive. And as a spouse, she clearly had opportunity. "Were you aware that Ms. Montoya was also found dead?"

A dark look passed over Mrs. Davenport's carefully constructed face. Unfortunately for Harsley's new theory, this new information was clearly a surprise. Either that or Ophelia belonged on the stage. "What are you talking about?"

Somewhere in the house, a thud sounded on the stairs. Harsley turned to face the foyer and met Amanda Pike's eyes. The chair of the Art Department froze in the doorway separating the two rooms for the briefest of moments. Ophelia stubbed out her cigarette in the ashtray.

"What are you doing here?" The anger in the professor's voice was somehow artificially commanding. It was as if she was practiced in making men squirm. Her eyes flashed dangerously as she walked into the room, taking the seat on the couch beside Mrs. Davenport. "I spoke to President Yaftali last night. This investigation is to be closed. Your ME found enough evidence to explain Eric's death as a suicide and the girl's as an unfortunate accident. You have no business bothering us."

"Amanda, why didn't you tell me that the girl Eric was sleeping with was dead?" There was genuine confusion in Ophelia's voice as she turned to the woman next to her, and Harsley's suspicion that she hated her husband enough to kill began to wane.

"I was trying to protect you, Ophelia. There wasn't any point in making you more upset," Pike stated sharply, her eyes never leaving Harsley's for a moment.

"Ms. Pike, I could easily ask what *you're* doing here. Is there a reason that you're at Mrs. Davenport's home at seven thirty in the morning?"

"Ophelia and I are close friends. It's not unusual for me to be in this house, especially lately, considering the circumstances. Are you telling me it's wrong to comfort a friend with a recently deceased husband, Detective?"

Harsley finished his cigarette and leaned across the coffee table to stub it out in the ashtray. He had to think quickly.

The Davenport home was the fanciest place Harsley had ever seen. Room after room was visible through a series of French doors, all of them elaborately decorated with settees and armchairs and rugs of colorful materials handwoven in intricate patterns. The focal point of the living room, however, was a marble fireplace above which hung an oversized oil portrait of Eric and Ophelia Davenport, dressed like royalty. Likely

the taste of the young Mrs. Davenport, who was now looking between her supposed friend and the detective, her eyes
taking on the shine of mounting distress. Yes, her home and
those gaudy weddings rings were statements, but they were
not statements of murder. Ophelia Davenport was not capable of these crimes. Harsley observed her manicured nails: she
wasn't the type to get her hands dirty.

Amanda Pike, however, had an investment in the conclusion
of this case. Her admitted close contact with Yaftali attested to that.
And as chair of the Art Department, she would likely have a taste
for the unusual. Who was to say that murder wasn't her medium?

"Ms. Pike, if you were aware of the fact that Eric Davenport
was having an affair with Ms. Montoya, would you be the
friend that Mrs. Davenport mentioned earlier? The one who
confirmed her suspicions?"

Pike took a deep breath, and her body seemed to expand
with agitation. A slight redness rushed to her cheeks, and Harsley
couldn't help but connect her inflated figure to the image of a
blowfish. "I didn't admit to knowing about Eric's relationship
with one of his students. I didn't know, not before the investigation," she snapped abruptly, clenching the armrest of the couch.

Time enough had passed. Harsley reached his conclusion,
even if he couldn't yet prove it. "I think you're full of shit," he
declared. "Ophelia all but ratted you out. I would start telling
the truth if I were you, Ms. Pike." He paused and leaned back in
his chair, hoping she would counter his bluff and inadvertently
reveal something she'd rather remain hidden.

Amanda Pike adjusted herself in her seat, shrinking back into the cushions as she kept a steady gaze on Harsley. She toyed with the collar of her blouse, flattening it before obsessively pulling at her sleeves. A slow, calculated smile spread across her face, accentuating the beginnings of wrinkles. The effort almost seemed to pain her. "I think we both know you're—what is that quaint policeman's phrase?—fishing."

"It must have made you angry," Harsley said, continuing to spool out his bait, leaning forward so his elbows were perched against his knees, "to see your friend taken advantage of. Especially when he had already done so much to you. To your department. The funding wasn't going to go to the arts. Where it deserved to be. Where it belonged."

Amanda nodded slightly, unconsciously, her jaw set. She exhaled heavily, the tenseness in her posture weakening. "Fine, I knew. And yes, I told her. Are you saying I should have kept that a secret from my friend?" Pike was starting to loosen. It would take only a little more pressure to break her down completely. Harsley needed to make her believe that he understood.

"I'm not saying that at all, Ms. Pike. He was a serial abuser of young women. First Mrs. Davenport here, and then Grace, a very promising art student. It was personal."

Amanda Pike shifted her weight to lean forward as if to deliver a long-winded, prepared lecture. An expression of joy flickered on her face for the briefest of moments. Then she cleared her throat and gave Harsley a look as if she wanted to watch him burn. "He deserved it," she said simply, her statement ending with a pause that hung in the silence, indicating that there was more to be said.

Her story was falling apart, leaving empty shells of excuses. It had to be her, Harsley decided. As a member of the art faculty, she had a strong interest in discrediting the Science and Math Departments. Orchestrating a friendship with the easily manipulated Ophelia Davenport gave her an insider's view of Eric Davenport's projects. Projects that might have jeopardized the Art Department's chances at funding or whatever it was that the people at this college were crazed about. And informing her about the mathematician's affair would be enough to win the spurned woman to Pike's cause.

In fact, Pike also had access to the art show, and the arrangement of those frames that formed the mysterious V pattern. The one that matched the marking on Grace's body. And that was on her own nape, according to that strange boy-detective, Ben. Everything came back to the woman sitting in front of him. He watched as she gritted her teeth, jaw set into a hard line. She would make a statement. Isn't that what all artists wanted?

"You know what I think, Ms. Pike? I think you killed Eric Davenport and Grace Montoya. I think you saw them as a threat. Mr. Davenport had the power to dismantle your department with his work. So you manipulated his wife into giving you information. You fed her what you knew about the affair and then you killed him. But that wasn't good enough, because then you got to thinking that maybe he told the girl something. Maybe she knew too much. So you killed her, too."

"Amanda." Ophelia Davenport's eyes widened and she stood, moving away from the couch where her friend sat.

"That's absolutely ridiculous. Do you hear yourself, Detective?"

"I do. You're under arrest for the murders of Eric Davenport and Grace Montoya." Harsley yanked Amanda Pike to her feet, pulling out a pair of handcuffs from his pocket before securing her wrists behind her.

"You're making a mistake!" Pike cried. "And I promise you, you'll pay. One way or another, you'll all pay."

CAITLIN MURPHY

24.

Simon bit down so hard he tasted blood. He had won just about every game of rock paper scissors he had played with Michael until now. He hated Michael and his stupid brains. His brother would go home and sleep like a rock, while Simon's life was about to be cut short. He and his abductors were only a few feet into the tunnel. He wondered which one of them was holding the gun.

Simon imagined his parents arranging his funeral. The community would probably hold a candlelight vigil and News 4 would be on-site. Pictures of his face before he started puberty would adorn memorial tee shirts like at a Bar Mitzvah. His old girlfriend, Mandy, would start cutting her wrists again. Michael would no longer be the favorite son: he'd be the kid who could never live up to his dead brother's legacy.

"Stop dragging your feet kid," one of his captors growled.

Simon felt the gun press into his back. He let out a cry that made him sound like a damsel in distress.

"Shit, dude, should we just do it?" the other thug asked the first.

"Now? We're not there yet."

"He's all squirmy, man."

They led Simon farther into the tunnel. Graffiti that he could barely make out covered the walls. Simon wondered who would bother to read it. The tags were scribbled on top of one another. Simon's own verbal vandalism occurred on classroom desks and bathroom stalls, where it had an audience, and he was proud of that. He was just beginning to be able to tell his two kidnappers apart. One was taller than the other; the taller one also had hair at the end of his chin, a goatee. The tunnel appeared to spin around him and the light ahead danced teasingly. Pitchy moans and hums began to echo from the distance. Simon's eyelids grew heavy, and he dragged his feet. He tried asking what the noise was, but his words melted together.

They reached an archway where the tunnel widened. A crowd of hooded figures in dim candlelight sang long and sleepy notes. Everything seemed to spin. Simon wondered if someone was going to be sacrificed, or if a heart was going to be savagely torn out of a living chest. His stomach retaliated at the thought of human organs.

He tried to jerk his wrists from the clammy grip, but it was unbreakable and he hung his head and sobbed. His newfound glimmers of manhood were dwindling fast. All men let the macho façade go when they stand helpless in front of a gun. Simon had seen it happen in the movies that he and his dad watched together. The guy about to die always blubbered about his kids and his wife. But trying to sway the shooter never worked. Still, Simon fell into the exact same trap. "I'm just a kid!" he yelped, "I'm fourteen and I wanna pass my English test next week. C'mon man."

"You 'c'mon.' We're nearly ready." The big man aimed the gun directly into Simon's mouth.

"Please," Simon whined. "I'm only fourteen. I'm still a vir—" Suddenly, he felt a painful burn in the back of his throat.

The assailants laughed, and the shooter put the gun into his own mouth and pulled the trigger again. Then he shook his head and declared, "Good stuff."

"C'mon, let me have some," his friend complained.

"All things come to them who wait."

"Not if you finish the Jack first."

Whiskey. The weapon was a water gun filled with whiskey

"You want any more, kid?" said the big guy.

Simon was stunned, then realized two options confronted him: he could run home to bed, or he could take this first-in-a-lifetime opportunity to get drunk. "Yeah, gimme some more," he said. They handed him the gun, and he happily sprayed another jet of the harsh, strangely sweet stuff into his open mouth. The liquor burned his throat and simmered at the bottom of his stomach. Trying to play it cool, he took another shot. "What the hell is this about?" he asked, handing the gun back.

"Well, we've got this school project."

The music loomed, or Simon was finally able to perceive it, an eerie keening that seemed to come from the tunnel's damp walls.

"Yeah, and this is the only way we can get an audience. We're music majors. We primarily study medieval music, and this is our senior thesis on the Gregorian chant. We're doing it down here 'cause the acoustics are perfect."

"But . . ." Simon wanted to ask why they couldn't just put a flyer on the blue light pole like everyone else.

"According to this study I read, the combination of shock and terror with the experience of the chant causes a chemical reaction that results in a sense of revelation. We started doing this routine last year. Sometimes people get pissed off, but once we give them the booze it's cool. No one's ever reported us. Even with all the murders on campus. Actually, it kind of makes it more fun, 'cause everyone's on their toes. More?" He held out the gun.

"Hell yeah!"

MATTIE HAGERTY

25.

Carl gazed absent-mindedly around the Art Department waiting room, took a sip of his coffee, and grimaced. Damn, he thought, you'd think at a college this expensive they'd at least have good coffee. It was appallingly bitter and included a sharp, earthy flavor that was altogether foreign to him. The barista at the student center had poured it generously, contradicting her outward appearance of apathy and disdain. Not only was the cup so thin the heat seared his fingers on the walk over to the art building, but the flap in the plastic cover wouldn't close once opened so that gouts of scalding hot liquid splashed onto Carl's already smarting hand. He took another sip and considered abandoning the cup on the fire extinguisher set into a wall niche like a Joseph Cornell box.

The door to Miriam Aarons's office swung open, and a petite, expensively dressed girl made her way into the waiting room. Her eyes appeared to be lined with black chalk. She wore fingerprint-smeared, thick-rimmed glasses that looked suspiciously non-prescription and had three piercings in her left eyebrow and too-long bangs that hung down over her face.

Despite the distracting and obscuring quantity of her facial adornment, she seemed genuinely upset, her cheeks having the semi-inflated look people get when they've been holding back tears. Carl gazed beyond her and made eye contact with Miriam Aarons, who sat placidly at her desk, framed by the open doorway.

"I'll be with you in a moment, Mr. Baker." She held up one finger without smiling. "Angela, please close the door behind you."

The girl named Angela jerked the door shut, and half-sat, half-flung herself into a cheaply cushioned IKEA one-seater opposite Carl. Now the tears began to flow freely, creating gray and black smears that ran down her cheeks. For ten very awkward seconds, she and Carl stared at each other. He was unsure how to handle the situation, and Angela seemed bent on silently, passively dragging him down to the innermost ring of her personal misery. He opened his mouth to break the intolerable silence, but she beat him to it.

"I'm. Fine. Stop looking at me. Okay?"

"Okay," Carl replied quickly.

A moment passed, and then, without any provocation, Angela began to speak with forced exasperation, as though doing him a favor. "She's just a huge bitch, and her lecture is an excuse for her to get up on her high horse of art and culture and word-puke all over us. She knows that I'm a transfer student and that makes everything, like, *so much harder* for me and she doesn't give a damn! It's unfair, I, like, practically have a handicap in her class!"

Angela sighed so dramatically that Carl initially mistook it for wheezing. She stared at him, and he racked his mind for an appropriate comment. "I'm sorry?" he offered.

"Of course you are," she spat venomously. "I didn't ask for your sympathy, and I don't want your condolences. Classic male behavior, assuming you're the only one capable of providing the support a woman needs and, *oh, hurray,* you've saved me! Little, helpless me. . . . Well, screw you!"

She stood in a tiny, black cyclone of Dior handbag and fake glasses and marched toward the door that led to the hallway. As she passed out of the room, Carl heard her mutter, "Fucking men!"

The door to Miriam Aarons's office swung open.

"Please come in now," she said energetically. Carl did as he was told, and took a seat opposite her desk. He was tired and felt drained by the case and how convoluted it had become. Now he was grasping at straws.

"Sorry about that," Miriam began hastily, leaning almost conspiratorially across her desk. "Angela's a transfer student. Need I say more?"

Carl looked quizzically at her, wholly unsure what she was implying but able to catch on that it wasn't positive.

"What brings you to my office for the second time in less than a week?" she asked.

"To be honest, Dr. Aarons—"

"Miriam's fine," she offered this time.

"To be honest, Miriam, it's for a lack of anywhere better to be." He paused, missing the forthright swagger that typically buoyed him when he was pursuing a case. He was acutely aware of the unprofessionalism of his actions.

"Detective Harsley called last night to inform me that the investigation into the murders is over, and that I'm to assume the investigation of a new case promptly. I have a few days until we move on to the new case . . . and . . . well, the call just doesn't sit right for me. There are too many unanswered questions. Too many loose ends to tie up without additional help."

"Moi?" She shrugged.

"No, no, I'm not here to interrogate you. It's simply that you were close to Grace. Also, you are very familiar with the Art Department and its faculty. I thought that maybe you'd be willing to tell me a little more about Grace, about your department. And more about Amanda Pike, surely?"

She didn't answer, so he continued. "Can I ask: what's the real reason for the tension between the arts and sciences?"

"So, you're telling me that the case is closed, but you're still pursuing the investigation?"

Carl nodded.

"That's rather . . . extracurricular of you, isn't it?" A glint of light came into her eyes, and the small smile that had been politely tacked onto her face stretched a tiny bit wider.

"Well yes, you could say so." He brought up a chuckle. "Really, Miriam, I'm not here as a member of the force, but simply as myself." He patted his left hip, where the holster to his firearm usually hung. "Look Miriam, no arms."

Her smile grew into a full grin, "I'll admit, this does set me at ease, Mr. Baker. You asked about the tensions between the arts and sciences?"

Carl nodded.

She paused and when she began to speak, her tone had hardened. Carl felt, very slightly, intimidated.

"Let me be frank with you, the men that comprise the faculty of Underhill's Math and Science Departments—and they are ALL men—are fucking pigs."

Carl's eyes shot open at her uncharacteristic vulgarity. The atmosphere in the room grew cool, and the warm roundness was gone from Miriam's gaze.

"They're chauvinists," she stated, as though she was waiting for him to agree. He didn't respond, so she continued. "It goes beyond the Math and Science Departments and their building. This is about men and women. The arts at Underhill have long enjoyed a prestigious reputation and held to an uncompromising standard. And, if you haven't noticed, this department is headed by women. Indeed, women have been responsible for nearly every seminal work produced by this college as a whole. Have you heard of the article 'Anti-Numerical Degradations of Post-Modernist Discontents'?"

"Not that I know of . . ."

"Of course not, I shouldn't expect you to be aware of something that important in the history of academia. You can't help what you are." Carl was beginning to resent the way she talked down to him as if he were a freshman. Or a transfer.

"It's only one of the most significant intellectual theses in ultra-modern art history, Mr. Baker. Not only is it an act of pure, socio-intellectual semiosis, but it saved this school when it was published because of the attention, acclaim, and funding it brought in. That article was written by Amanda Pike, our very own division chair."

She stared at him, apparently waiting for a reaction. Carl had no idea how to respond, so he nodded and blankly held her gaze. She shook her head in disappointment.

"I'm saying that Amanda Pike is a genius, a brilliant scholar, a visionary, and yet all the credit, which you are obviously in the dark about, went to Winston Aberworth. *Winston fucking Aberworth*, who teaches cellular biology to sophomores. But because he's a man, and because he opened his loud mouth at the right time, he got all the credit! Amanda Pike got NONE!"

"Okay." Carl was beginning to doubt that Miriam Aarons would be able to help him with the investigation.

"Listen. The tension at Underhill College isn't about academic prodigality, understand? It's bigger than that. It's about the inherent worth of art, the wastefulness of the sciences and mathematics at this school, and above all, it's about gender."

Carl was beginning to feel lightheaded.

"Yes, gender! *Everything,* Mr. Baker, is about gender. And gender is, of course, about art. But we'll get to that. Consider this: every time the college sponsors a math class, we impose the socio-sexual masculinization of thought into our precious students. Every time we allow some naive and helpless fresh-woman to sign up for a class in calculus or statistics, we are forcing the heteronormativity of ingrained gender ideologies down her throat. Don't you get it? Numbers are deeply, irrevocably gendered, and we are subjecting our best and brightest to the hegemonic power structure of mathematics."

"What the hell are you talking about?" Carl asked, equally fascinated and repulsed by her bewildering fanaticism.

"Numbers are not innocent, detective. Numbers and their constituents stand to hurt people, to maim them, to disempower them, and to strip them of their emotional, intellectual, and most importantly, sexual freedom. And numbers, at this school and beyond, are a man's game. Why, I ask, is the phallus the symbol for the positive number one while the vagina represents zero. Nothing. Just like the late Eric Davenport and his games of chess—recall what he taught? Mathematics! Numbers are the undeniable icons of masculine intellectualism, and I will not stand for their suffocating effect on the lives and academic pursuits of young women. Don't get me wrong, I am no shepherd, and I am not protecting my 'flock.' No, I am restoring an ancient balance, and it is decidedly female. Think of me as the curator of a very, very important museum. Occasionally, I must take an inventory of my acquisitions, and remove the pieces that no longer fit. By carefully pruning the weak, subversive, and disastrous elements, my gallery will retain its beauty, its power. Let me show you an example of just such a disaster. Look at this monstrous building they plan to erect. An edifice devoted to math and masculinity!"

Miriam unrolled one of the documents that Carl had thought was a poster on her desk and spread it out for him to inspect. For a moment, he couldn't get his eyes to focus. When they did, he saw they it was the blueprint for a building that was, he thought, elegant.

"Tasteless!" Miriam snapped. "Tasteless and shameless. The damn thing looks like a cock!"

Carl couldn't suppress his laugh. "I don't see it."

"You don't? Look here, how it juts out of the earth, rising skyward like some triumphant spire. It's hideous."

Carl sighed, growing steadily less comfortable in her office. He felt too hot, and a bit faint. He would not have been surprised at Miriam's eclectic side or even a certain moodiness, for she was deeply involved in the arts at a notoriously liberal college. However, this was becoming unpleasant.

Before he could begin to escape the conversation and slip out of her office, he noticed something scribbled in green on the corner of one of the blueprints. Only half of the scribble was visible, the rest obscured by another architectural drawing, but Carl instantly recognized the green *V* that had been so ubiquitous it might have stood for Underhill if the school's name had been carved in stone. VNDERHILL.

"Miriam, tell me about this," He pointed to the green mark. His eyes scanned her face for a reaction.

"Why, have you seen it before?" She glanced casually at the blueprint.

"No," he hemmed.

"Well then, you're either stupid or a liar." Her grin returned in full. Carl felt disoriented and registered her insult, though he couldn't seem to respond. She began to roll the papers back into a tube.

Carl could have sworn he heard her mutter, "Both, it seems."

"Wha—?" was all he could muster.

"Good question, detective." She spoke as if presenting an old lecture to a new class. "The *V* that you see is, in fact, an *M*."

She pulled up her sleeve and showed him the green tattoo he had noticed on their first encounter. It was indeed an *M*, the second half of it having been covered when he glimpsed it a few days ago. It occurred to him that the other *V*s he had seen, in the art show and on Grace Montoya's neck, might have been *M*s too.

"The *M* stands for Mona, which is, naturally, a reference to the famous painting by the artist commonly known as Leonardo da Vinci."

"So what?"

"Listen!" She reprimanded him. "When da Vinci recorded something important, he wrote it backward. In this way, the artist was secretive and cunning. Any good art historian knows that to understand dead artists, she must get inside their heads. So, let us consider Leonardo da Vinci's work backward. And what was his ultimate work? The *Mona Lisa*. Thus, we necessarily look at 'Mona Lisa' backward. Are you following me, detective?"

"Uhh . . . right."

"Keep up. 'Mona Lisa' backward is Asil Anom. A-S-I-L has no relevant translations in any of the ancient languages, and cannot be reduced to an iconic or textual representation of an artistic theme. But A-N-O-M, on the other hand, *does* hold some meaning. In day-to-day life, da Vinci spoke an antiquated version of Italian, but as a scholar he could most assuredly read and write in Latin. As you are obviously not a scholar of dead languages, detective, allow me to educate you.

"In Latin," she continued, "'A' means 'by' and 'Nom' means 'name.' In other words, 'Anom' translates into 'by the name of.' Leonardo da Vinci had been writing this, albeit backward, the whole time."

She stopped, looking at Carl expectantly. When no response came, she clicked her nails on the desk and sighed. "Come now, connect a few dots, will you?" Her voice dripped with condescension.

Carl struggled to follow her logic. "'Mona' means 'by the name of.' . . . Mona. Lisa. . . . By the name of Lisa? Are you saying that the title, 'Mona Lisa' is actually how Leonardo da Vinci was signing his work?"

"Yes, keep going." She grinned.

"Which would mean . . . that 'Leonardo' was a pen name, that in fact his name was *Lisa* . . . da Vinci?"

"Which implies . . ."

"That the famous painter was a woman?"

"Exactly!" she roared, startling him. "That's exactly it! The greatest, most fundamental, most preeminent and seminal works of art in the entirety of history were wrought by a woman's hands!"

Carl couldn't swallow it, but he wasn't given the chance to try.

"Do you realize what this means, detective? This turns the masculine structuralization of power in all of art on its head! This uproots the hegemony of phallicized institutional knowledge-making! This shatters the preconception that radical semiotics only trickle down from the top of the patriarchal power pyramid."

Jesus Christ, Carl thought in exasperation. I feel like I've got the worst hangover of my life.

"Miriam! What are you talking about?!"

"I'm telling you that this *M* stands for Mona, and that Mona is the proof that men aren't necessary for greatness, that women like Lisa da Vinci are the sole architects of genius, and that this college—this world—doesn't need men! At all! I am a crusader, Mr. Baker. And while I abhor genocide in any form, I do value a careful, calculated purge. It cannot be executed clumsily or without grace. Indeed, it requires the touch of an artist. Just like the curator of an important, aging gallery, I intend to trigger the metamorphosis that Underhill needs. We will finally evolve this school—and someday, all schools—to an all-girls environment, the way it was always meant to be! I will rid this institution of its rotten core: men!"

Carl was extremely dizzy, his thoughts were scattered, and he felt close to vomiting. He stood up wobbling, and turned unsteadily for the door.

His hand had barely touched the knob when she said softly, "That is why I killed Grace Montoya."

*

"God damnit, Harsley!" his captain yelled exactly four inches away from his face. "You are not the fucking Lone Ranger! You can't arrest anyone you like! Do you know how much flack I'm going to get and how much shit I'm going to eat because of this Pike woman? Her boss is fucking Mara Yaftali! AKA the largest employer in the county. She's got more friends in high places than Oprah's got free cars!"

"Sir! Please, just give me twenty minutes with the prisoner." Harsley hated many things, but there was nothing he hated more than begging.

The captain laughed. Everyone at the station was staring at them. "Dispatch contacted her husband while you were bringing her in, you idiot. *He was with her the night that man was murdered! At a charity dinner with the fucking mayor!*"

"I know, I know! It doesn't look good, but just let me ask her a few questions. There are leads that her husband's story doesn't rule out. Give me twenty minutes. Ten. If I'm wrong, I'll turn in my badge and gun voluntarily."

His captain took a step forward and began speaking under his breath so that no one else could hear. "I fucking hate you, Harsley. I'm sick of putting my ass on the line. Now, we both know you're too fucking good to throw in the gutter, so why don't you grow a goddamn pair and stop limp-dickin' me around. I'm gonna give you five minutes with her, and if you get nothing, I'm assigning your ass to Howland county for the rest of the year."

Harsley didn't hesitate and headed toward the interrogation room. Yet, the more he thought about the situation, the more he was sure he'd made the wrong decision. Yes, cuffing Amanda Pike kept up the pressure, but since Hurst Green's duly elected mayor refuted the sheer oversimplicity of Harsley's accusation, he was certain the art historian couldn't have been behind the Underhill killings. Though the detective's guts told him she was implicated—the woman reeked of malevolent intentions—there was no way she could have committed the killings by herself.

That didn't mean, however, that there weren't questions that she might be able to shed light on. Nor, for that matter, did reassignment mean that he couldn't continue to pursue the case without his badge and gun.

Harsley waited for the door to the interrogation room to open. The captain stood behind him, breathing down his neck. The lock clicked loudly, and before Harsley entered the room, his boss growled, "I'm going to be watching on the monitor. If you have a scrap of dignity left in you, don't fuck this up anymore. Apologize to the woman and leave."

Harsley entered the white-walled room and sat down across the table from a very unhappy college professor.

"My boss asked me to say I'm sorry." Harsley let the words float off his tongue with as much sarcasm as he had could muster. "So, I'm sorry, Amanda."

"Screw you."

"Maybe later? I honestly don't care."

"Fucker! I'm going to personally ensure that Mara Yaftali has your head."

"I'm sure. First question. Are you aware of a network of tunnels that runs underneath your school?"

Pike looked at him as though he had three eyeballs. "Of all the questions you could ask me so that you might actually save your ass, this?"

"Please answer the question." He rolled his eyes at her.

"Yes. I am aware of the *tunnel*. It is not a *network*, it is a single tunnel, and it is what remains of an aborted municipal project to redirect a water main from campus to neighboring homes. What the hell, detective?"

He ignored her last question. "Are you aware that we've received reports of people using the tunnel for ritual purposes, including but not limited to incantations?"

"In fact, I'm not surprised at all. I have an advisee who asked permission to use the tunnel for a performance art project. It's ongoing, so it's not unreasonable, and the chanting isn't a shock either, because his piece is titled, 'Reinventing the Gregorian Chant: A Dialectic Introspection into Medieval Singing.' So again, detective, what the hell?"

"I should ask you that," he muttered.

Harsley opened his mouth to ask another question, but was cut off as the door swung open and his captain barked at him to get out.

Harsley complied, and smiled to himself as he heard the beginnings of what would probably be a long and groveling apology on his behalf by the captain. He didn't bother confronting his superior officer. He just stared at the floor and made his way to his car. He got in, turned the AC on full blast, and pulled a cigarette out from his shirt pocket. He rolled the tip between his fingers, and then lit it. The first drag is the best, he thought as he pulled out of the lot and headed back toward Hurst Green.

But not the school. Nearby. The only place he hadn't fully investigated.

The driveway to the Davenport residence was a deep swath of cobblestones embedded in dark concrete, girded on both sides by lush green grass, which was in turn walled in by dense, perfectly shaped boxwoods. The clean air hit his lungs and made him cough. Ophelia stood in the doorway.

"Back so soon, detective?" she purred. She wore a brilliant, bright red dress that sloped from her shoulders down to her ankles. Decidedly more composed than she was when we left this morning, Harsley noted.

He strode up to her, cheeks flushed, and pulled out another cigarette. "Got a light?"

"Of course." She lit his Camel. "Come in. You want some coffee? It's *Torrefaction*." She rolled the *r*'s halfway to Detroit.

Police axiom #1: Never refuse a beverage.

Police axiom #2: Especially if it's offered by a beautiful woman.

"Well, I'm not one to make a lady insist," he said, vibrantly aware of the sexual potential of this encounter. She left for the kitchen, gesturing Harsley toward a chair in the living room. He admired her derriere as she walked away from him.

Perfection, he mused wistfully.

In the time it had taken Harsley to shuttle Amanda Pike to the station, get reamed by his boss, question Pike for five minutes, and then drive back, Ophelia had removed every single bouquet, basket, and pot of flowers from the living room. Without them, the room was cavernously huge and the daylight streaming through the windows illuminated the furnishings with a brightness that seared Harsley's eyes. He noticed that the smoke from his cigarette was the only uncontained, asymmetrical, and chaotic texture in the entire room. From somewhere beneath the floor, he heard a strange clanking.

"What's making that noise?" Harsley asked as Ophelia gracefully sailed back into the room, two steaming cups of black coffee in her hand.

"Oh, it's the house's ancient heating system. It's louder than Mjölnir."

Harsley stared blankly at her. "Louder than what?"

"Mjölnir . . . Thor's hammer. Norse god of thunder? Not ringing any bells?"

Harsley just stared at her.

"Well, that's what I get for choosing a liberal arts education. Anyway, you can't hear the boiler upstairs. Otherwise, it would keep me awake at night. I'm a girl who needs her serenity."

"I can appreciate that," Harsley murmured, trying to keep his voice both feather-soft and seductive. "Listen, I didn't mean to scare you by arresting Amanda Pike earlier, and if it's any comfort, everything didn't go according to—"

"I don't want to hear another word. If there is something I should know about Amanda, I'd rather she tell me herself.

We are very close, and I am still a little sensitive to receiving bad news from the lips of policemen. So, please. Good news, or interesting questions only." Her smile had returned.

He sipped his coffee and sat back, thoroughly enjoying the flirtatious atmosphere. He was also surprised at how much he enjoyed the coffee she had poured for him. It was light, sharp, and had a natural sweetness. It had another flavor, however, that Harsley couldn't place. "Where's this from?" he asked.

Ophelia rolled her eyes dramatically. "Oh, I don't know. Eric was the connoisseur. I just like it." She paused and then asked playfully, "So? Tell me, why are you here? I simply won't believe you if you tell me it's simply for my company."

"As much as I hate to mix business with pleasure . . ." He winked at her. "I do have a few questions."

"Fire away, Detective, fire away."

Harsley squinted. The room seemed to be growing brighter.

"I wanted to ask you about Eric. Amanda Pike and I talked about a series of tunnels that may run underneath the campus. She said that there was, in fact, only one tunnel, but I have a map that—"

"Jesus H. Christ! Eric died, but his tunnels prevail," Ophelia blurted out.

Harsley looked at her, wholly bemused. "Go on."

"He was fanatical about them. Chess first, math second, and holy hell if it wasn't the tunnels third! They were his pet project, his obsession. And, of course, if you were so much as a transfer student here, you'd know by the end of your first semester that the tunnels were a joke. They're where kids

would smoke a joint before hitting the parties. But to Eric, the
tunnels were Plato's cave from which he could never climb
out. He put together drawing after drawing of them from the
bullshit he'd pry out of his less-than-sober advisees."

"You don't say," Harsley said softly. He was satisfied at
how coherent that made some of his intuitions. The brightness
of the room had blossomed into a headache directly behind
his eyes.

"So it would be reasonable to expect that Mr. Davenport
might have tried to convince others of these tunnels?"

Ophelia guffawed, "Others? Try anyone who would listen. He'd pawn off pages from his journal to strangers on the
street." She paused, taking a sip of coffee and lighting another
cigarette. Then, in a more reflective tone, she observed, "You
know, I shouldn't be so critical. You can't blame Eric for half
the crazy stuff he did when he was alive. It's not as if he was
entirely well in the head."

Harsley's detective senses picked this line up like a shark
smelling blood in the water. "What do you mean, exactly?"

"I don't mean to say he was actually crazy. He was a genius
in his field, no doubt, but he wasn't very healthy by the time
he died. He had kidney stones, and he suffered from chronic
muscle spasms. It made his voice and his breathing shaky. But
. . ." She trailed off.

"But?" Harsley echoed.

"But I can't help but wonder if all the health issues affected
his thinking. He wasn't always cogent. Like, right before he
died, he kept talking about a gambit, whatever that is. And

before that, it was a soliloquy, and before that, a neopet. I don't know what half these things are. I don't think anyone did, except for Eric. And he'd know *everything* about them, and find ways to apply them to his life. They were his little puzzle pieces that would fit for two, maybe three days, and then he'd move on. That isn't normal thinking, you know?" Ophelia's tone had darkened, growing more rueful. She had brought her mug up to her face. Harsley's head pounded. The light in this room is too fucking bright! he thought.

He sought to change directions and talk about someone else. "What about Eva? Did he have anything to do with her?"

Ophelia choked on her coffee, and her eyes narrowed. "That bitch! Why do you want to know about her?"

"I . . . I was just curious," Harsley stammered. His head throbbed, and he brought his hand up to his brow, the ash at the tip of his cigarette toppling onto the white couch. He grimaced and tried to wipe it off.

"Oh gosh, stop that. I'll have the maid deal with it," Ophelia said calmly. "I didn't mean to freak you out. I just don't have much good will toward Ms. Valdez."

Harsley let a long moment go by in silence. "Can I ask why?"

She sighed dramatically. "Eva has . . . well, she has everything. She has money; she has houses; she has cars; she has diamonds. Eva has a husband in Paris, Tokyo, New York, and Amsterdam. And those are the ones she talks about. Who knows how many other men she has tucked away around the world?"

"What? How?" Harsley asked, intrigued. Also confused. He was sweating profusely and brought up a hand to wipe his

brow. It didn't occur to him that Ophelia didn't seem overheated at all.

"What do you mean, how? Her daddy's company that she
inherited when she was sixteen. Valdez Pharmaceuticals ring
a bell?"

Holy shit, Harsley thought as his head pounded. Of course.
Why didn't I realize that?

"So is that what Mrs. Yaftali meant when she introduced
Eva as 'a good friend of the school?'" He was panting slightly
now, trying to quell the rising nausea.

"Probably, considering how much damn money she's
donated."

"But wait, why would she have an interest in Underhill?"
he asked, breathing heavily.

"My God, detective, how do you make a paycheck each
month? Put it all together. Eric wasn't a faithful man! By the
time he died, he had a wife plus some witless sophomore he
was screwing on the side. Guess who I used to be?" For the first
time she sounded pathetic.

"A sophomore that Eric Davenport had an affair with . . .
when he was married to Eva Louisa Valdez?" Harsley asked
in disbelief. Everything in the room had blurred to an opaque
whiteness, except for Ophelia's absurd red dress.

"Bingo," she responded without enthusiasm.

"Which makes Eric . . ."

"A manslut!" Ophelia hissed. Harsley couldn't remain in
her stifling, white living room anymore. He had to get outside
and get fresh air. He lurched to his feet and managed to stand

for a full second before Ophelia rose and pushed him roughly back down into the couch.

"Sit!" she commanded, causing more dizziness to cascade over him. He felt as though his limbs were cast in lead. From somewhere under the coffee table, Ophelia brought out a roll of duct tape.

KIT HOWLAND

26.

Carl stopped but didn't let go of the doorknob.

"What did you say?" he asked, swaying. His eyes couldn't focus, and his center of gravity felt inverted.

"Come back here, detective. There's more I want to share with you. You'll find the door is locked, anyway."

Sure enough it was, and all too quickly Carl had to decide between sitting back down in the chair opposite Miriam Aarons or falling to the floor. He sat, trying to focus his eyes on her. In between blinks, he could barely distinguish her blurry outline.

"Let's be *real* with each other, as my advisees say. While the coffee here at Underhill is woefully terrible, yours probably tasted particularly bad, yes? That's because I had your beverage dosed with this."

She pulled a small, crystal vial of transparent green fluid from her pocket, and set it on the desk between them.

"You . . . you poisoned me?" Carl eventually slurred.

"Technically, no. I had Sarah Florence, the barista at the student center, do it," she said frankly. "Detective, this is a class one nerve agent. It is derived from a particular hormone found in a single species in the animal kingdom: the praying mantis. This hormone is responsible for the mantis's most characteristic behavior: the female's consumption of the male after coitus. What you drank is a condensed form of the mantis hormone. In a small dose, such as I gave you, it causes partial paralysis, photosensitivity, disorientation, head pain, and maybe nausea. Such a dose also makes the user extremely susceptible to suggestion. Tremendous, isn't it, how much alike this agent is to subliminal content in post-postmodern art? Ironically, in a medium dose the effect is quite the opposite: it acts as an aphrodisiac, inciting the user to fornicate with desperation."

She paused, dropping the vial into her pocket. "Here's where it gets interesting, however. If someone is subjected to a heavy dose of the substance—say, in a gaseous form—the victim passes through the aphrodisiac stage and slips into a homicidal mania. Literally, the user will try to mate with someone, anyone, and thereafter kill them."

"That's sick." Carl uttered, the fog persisting both in his head and before his eyes.

"It's not sick, detective, it's miraculous." Miriam Aarons's voice had lost its earlier fervor and was now deadly calm. "This nerve agent is the tool of my mission, the sword in my crusade. With this, I will purify Underhill. It heralds retribution for all the unforgivable acts of selfishness, greed, and brutality that the male faculty of Underhill College have committed over the years. I am an artist, and this is my medium."

"Grace. She was your first victim?" Carl asked, breathing heavily.

"Grace was my protégée! I taught her everything she knew, and she saw the beauty in my vision for this school. She was elected to carry out the first mission. We'd been routing shipments of mantises for extraction through the school to avoid suspicion. Even the student who delivered the biomass via a hidden tunnel didn't know what was happening. But Davenport grew suspicious. Combine that with his role on the Science Center Committee and the solution was obvious."

"You're heinous."

Miriam ignored him and kept up her happy recitation. "So we gave Grace an early batch of the mantis hormone to ease her morals and her scruples. Unfortunately, Eva hadn't yet perfected the formula."

Carl's eyes flickered in recognition.

"So the effects didn't wear off the way we thought it would. Grace succeeded in her mission to kill Davenport, but she never fully returned from the experience. She became pathologically obsessed with carrying out Underhill's transformation and started stealing the insects and using them for her own purposes. Stupid ideas, that girl had! She found joy in ruining art, not making it. She started seducing people left and right—even her poor, witless roommate! Put simply, she became a liability. So, I did what was necessary, and put her down. We all have to make sacrifices for the greater good, you know.

"Of course, arranging an accident would have been wasteful. We needed to make an example out of Grace, to use her to discipline and educate future initiates. After all, the first artwork always makes the biggest splash."

Carl tried to answer, to throw some curse or inflammatory remark at her, but his mouth was filled with cotton.

"Oh, my, I've probably talked your ears off, haven't I? Well, correct me if I'm wrong, but there's somewhere more important for you to be, isn't there? Francesca!" she called.

Through the dimness swallowing his vision, Carl saw a huge form coming toward him from the doorway. As it got closer, he realized it was a massive, human hulk in full security uniform. The name stitched to the guard's gigantic chest read, "FRANK." Carl passed out.

*

Kate woke with a gasp. She felt as though she had been holding her breath for a month. She looked around, disoriented.

Where the fuck am I?

She tried to move and found that her arms and hands were bound together above her head. She tried to kick, but her feet were secured tightly as well. Beginning to panic, Kate twisted left and thrashed right, but the only effect of her effort was the sound of chain links clinking together. Then it all came back to her.

After her phone call with Harsley, she had drifted about her apartment, groggy and agitated for no discernible reason. She kept attempting to rationalize her message to him. Indeed, it had seemed paramount that the case be called off, but for the life of her she couldn't figure out why. The closest sensation she could compare her condition to was coming down from the few and infrequent cocaine-fueled benders she had experienced in college.

Mara Yaftali had shown up at her apartment the next morning. She brought coffee, insisting that they had made brunch plans the previous day. Kate remembered feeling skeptical but let her in, hoping that Mara might be able to explain her daze. She remembered taking a few large gulps of the coffee and that it had tasted slightly off. Then nothing.

Kate took a deep breath.

Okay . . . I've been drugged. But I've got to get it together. There might not be much time.

She looked around at the room, which was brightly lit with fluorescent bulbs. Along the wall to her left stood a series of massive brass tanks connected by a network of thick rubber tubes. Each tank had a panel of gauges and meters and a green ring that appeared to seal it. Across the room a large medical table held all manner of beakers, tubes, vials, and instruments. Also, there was a small, perhaps two-foot-square, steel door set into the wall.

I'm in some kind of . . . laboratory? What the hell?

She rolled over onto her right shoulder and gasped. Lying beside her, motionless, was Harsley. His hands and feet were bound with duct tape, and there was duct tape over his mouth.

She cried out his name, only to realize she herself had a wad of fabric stuffed in her mouth underneath half a roll of tape. She watched the detective's still form for the rise and fall of breath. Seeing it, she heaved a sigh of relief.

All right, girl, do something.

Kate reached up with both hands and probed her hairline for one of the bobby pins she used daily. She found one buried deep in her curly, auburn hair and insinuated it into the lock securing the chains that ran around her wrists. She had never actually practiced picking. At best, she had the vaguest idea of what she had to do.

This is bullshit, these are modern locks. They didn't come from a high school hallway.

She moaned, cursing the futility of her efforts.

She heard a door open and voices drifted down from somewhere above. She noticed for the first time a staircase leading into the lab. She palmed the bobby pin.

I must be in a basement.

The voices grew closer, and through the hair that fell over her eyes, Kate saw three women and a very large figure carrying a heavy, lumpy object wrapped in a blanket. The figure lurched up to her, and Kate quickly shut her eyes, pretending that she was still unconscious. A body was dumped behind her, and the footsteps climbed back up the staircase. Kate instantly recognized the cologne of the new body. Carl.

She risked cracking an eyelid again. Harsley stared back at her with bloodshot eyes. She raised her eyebrows in surprise. Harsley winked.

*

Miriam Aarons, Eva Louisa Valdez, and Mara Yaftali sat at a lab table across the room from their prisoners. Beethoven—*Eroica*—was playing from a nearby stereo, and they were sipping sherry while the enormous guard sat in the corner slugging

PBRs. Before them sat an ancient slide projector pointing at a blank wall.

"Ladies," Miriam Aarons addressed her companions. "We are now ready to initiate the second and final installment of our plan. Soon, we shall carve the masculine filth from Underhill campus like rot from an apple. No longer will the men of academia claim the glory that is ours by right! Once Amanda arrives, we will decide what to do with these three . . . interventionists." She flicked a wrist toward the prisoners who lay as if etherized upon the laboratory table. "Then, the path to liberation will be clear. Underhill shall become an all-girls school!"

The women murmured in agreement.

"Until then, I have a very special presentation to show you. It's a collection of my most recent findings regarding the female origins of ancient art technique. I shouldn't have to tell you that *no one* has seen these slides yet."

"Oooh! How exciting, Miriam!" Mara Yaftali exclaimed. Eva sighed but otherwise remained silent. Miriam turned on the projector, walked quickly to a switch by the staircase, and shut off the fluorescents. The light of the slides on the wall was sufficient to illuminate the three women, but it left the rest of the room shrouded in darkness. As the *Eroica* reached its climax, Miriam started talking animatedly. Her words were multisyllabic and largely incomprehensible.

Harsley was quietly trying to work his hands free of the tape. Yet Ophelia knew how to tie a man up. Despite his best efforts, his hands grew number, not freer. He gritted his teeth in frustration.

Suddenly, a new hand, cool and deliberate, tapped his shoulder and a soft, young voice whispered into his ear. "Don't move, Detective. I'm cutting you loose." He had heard the voice before . . . somewhere. He racked his brain. Slowly it came to him: the dead girl's angsty roommate—Imogen! He felt the tension around his ankles release, and the tape covering his mouth was gently peeled away.

"Cut the tape on my wrists, then free the other detective," he whispered.

"Already ahead of you. He's just waking up." She snipped the tape trapping his forearms together.

"How the hell did you find us?" Harsley couldn't help but ask.

"The tunnel, dumbo. I brought the mantises here from campus every week. Discretion, y'know?"

"What?" Harsley whispered.

"Shhh. I'll explain later. Don't try to follow me, you won't fit. Good luck."

He heard her shift quietly away from him and disappear into the small door that led to the tunnel. As if on cue, another door swung open, and Harsley watched as Amanda Pike descended into the laboratory. At the bottom of the staircase, she flipped on the lights. Behind her was Ophelia Davenport.

Eva Valdez immediately rose, her face set grimly. "What the *fuck* is this bitch doing here?" She glared murderously at Ophelia.

"Eva, dear, there's been a change of plans," Miriam said gently.

"You told me she was out of the picture by now!"

"I'm about to phase her out, Eva. The rest of our plan doesn't include her."

"That's not good enough, Miriam. We agreed that you'd destroy her. She's supposed to be dead."

"You told her *what*?" Ophelia cried. Her eyes adopted the round terror of a panicking mare.

"We can't just kill her. Ophelia's death would serve no purpose." Miriam tried to come across as soothing and commanding at the same time, but she sounded weak and worried instead. "She is the reason Detective Harsley is our prisoner."

"Oh, please, I could have had his head with a snap of my fingers. But this bitch, oh no, you said to keep my hands off, that you'd take care of her. Well, Miriam, where is Ophelia's final stroke?"

"What is she talking about?" Ophelia backed toward the staircase.

"Her death is the only reason I've been playing this stupid game. Do you think I give a damn about this creepy bug serum my scientists have been making for you?"

"Calm down, Eva, this isn't about you." Miriam's voice rose. Mara and Amanda had backed up to the wall, away from the table. Frank began to rouse from a six-pack slough.

"Yes, it is about me right now!" Eva roared at Miriam. "I want her out of the picture. NOW! Kill her right here, right now, or this whole charade ends."

For a tense moment, no one spoke.

Eva continued, "I am from Colombia! If I want someone dead, I feed them cyanide and keep it simple! But, for some

reason, she is still breathing. This . . . *witch* took my husband—
my MAN! And she couldn't even keep him! She deserves to
DIE!"

"Screw you!" screamed Ophelia as she turned to flee up
the staircase. Eva pulled a small handgun out of her snakeskin
purse and aimed it at her nemesis's back.

"Eva, no!" Miriam yelled, but it was too late.

The moment Eva squeezed the trigger, Harsley leaped forward and grabbed her arm. The bullet went askew and punctured the rubber tube leading into of one of the tanks lining the
wall adjacent to the staircase. Green tinted gas started hissing
out of the tank. Ophelia was knocked back by the force of the
release.

Holding his breath, Harsley shoved Eva aside and yanked the
small gun from her hand. He cracked the back of her head with
the butt, and then ran back to Carl and Kate.

"WHAT HAVE YOU DONE?" shrieked Miriam over the
vicious hiss of the tank. Gas quickly filled the room. The fumes
grew so thick they obscured the lights as Harsley tossed Kate
over his shoulder and yanked Carl to his feet.

Frank thundered across the room, but Kate managed to
kick the table into the path of the furious guard to buy them
additional seconds.

Together, they dashed and stumbled toward the staircase
and climbed out of the basement. Harsley shoved open the door
at the top of the stairs and threw Kate forward into the austere
white kitchen of chez Davenport. Carl leapt over her and Harsley
slammed the door shut. He gasped for air, keeping his weight

pressed against the door as one of the trapped women desper-ately attempted to push it open.

"LOCK IT!" He yelled at Carl, who quickly slid the bolt into place.

The banging on the other side quickly ceased, and for a few minutes, the basement was silent. All of the gas must have escaped from the tank, and it was likely too dark to see anymore.

Kate leaned against Harsley, breathing heavily. Carl sat a few paces away watching the door that Harsley slumped against.

They stared at each other, bewildered and panting, and none of them noticed as a faint trickle of green-tinted vapor seeped up from underneath the door.

Jarringly, Harsley's cell phone pinged with a text message. He grabbed it from his pocket without thinking. He didn't rec-ognize the number.

I DIDN'T KNOW IT THIS WAS FUCKED UP. I ONLY RESEARCHED THE NERVE HORMONE. THOUGHT MIRIAM WAS VISIONARY. PLEASE KEEP MY SECRET. I'LL KEEP YOURS.

WHAT SECRET? Harsley texted back, before he could stop himself.

His phone pinged back at him. YOU'LL SEE. OOPS, GOTTA GO. BEN'S WAITING. IN A CERTAIN LIGHT HE'S ALMOST CUTE.

After a few moments, they heard a new sound, a moan, only a moan, then several moans, which grew in frequency and fervor. The moans became groans, which became yelps, sighs, and unsuppressed cries of unmistakable eroticism. Harsley and Kate listened in disbelief, while Carl slowly realized what they were hearing.

"It's the nerve gas. Miriam explained it to me before I went under. We don't want to keep listening," he said quietly.

Harsley looked at him strangely, in a way Carl had never seen Harsley look at him. It was a look full of . . . yearning.

"No . . . I don't think I do," said Harsley softly.

"Me neither," purred Kate, beginning to grind her head into Harsley's lap.

"Having tasted his coffee, I bet Eric Davenport didn't withhold when it came to buying beds," Harsley said, starting to giggle without knowing why. Both Carl and Kate glanced at him quizzically. Then, they, too, began to laugh. It was a warm, mutual laughter, the kind lovers share.

Harsley took a deep breath and sighed. He reached down and stroked Kate's face. He loved her breasts, her perfect proportions. He looked at Carl, noticing for the first time how wonderfully accentuated his lips were, and how perfectly his shirt defined his chest. He took their hands, and began to lead them upstairs. He had no idea and didn't care what his motive was, but he had means and opportunity.

"Come on, I need a happy ending."

KIT HOWLAND

About the Authors

Sura Antolín is a senior at Sarah Lawrence College, studying creative writing and religion. She grew up in Evanston, Illinois, where at the age of five she began her first, still unfinished novel.

David Calbert is a recent graduate of Sarah Lawrence, where he concentrated in creative writing and literature. He has been writing for many years and hopes to pursue a career in it. David is originally from California. In New York he learned that cockroaches of enormous size exist and that they do not fear man-shrieking. This is David's first published work of fiction.

Madeline Dessanti recently graduated from Sarah Lawrence College. She hails from Teaneck, New Jersey, and enjoys playing tennis and meditating. She plans on entering a training program to become an American Sign Language interpreter.

Elliot Goldman has written from an early age. He is originally from Massachusetts but currently attends Sarah Lawrence

College with a concentration in art. Often writing in the absurd, he tends to focus on fantastical events. *Naked Came the Post-Postmodernist* is his first published work.

Jacqui Goodman is from Toronto and is into napping and things that smell nice. She is currently looking for a job in film (hire me!).

Mattie Hagerty is from Washington, D.C., and is a recent graduate of Sarah Lawrence College, where she concentrated in literature.

Jessye Holmgren-Sidell is from Chapel Hill, North Carolina. A college sophomore, she enjoys long walks in the park and extended games of Monopoly.

Kit Howland is an aspiring designer from Lincoln, Massachusetts. He's based in New York City and is currently looking for a job. If you've got one, let's talk.

Kelsey Joseph is a writer of stories and screenplays in Los Angeles, California.

Caitlin Murphy is an undergraduate fiction student from Ramsey, New Jersey. Currently a junior at Sarah Lawrence College, she has also been studying the art of professional daydreaming. The majority of her time is spent with her cats in a house by the sea.

Sasha Pezenik was born and raised in New York City. She is a hot-sauce fiend and recent graduate of Sarah Lawrence. She is a published author whose passion for writing and language provides her with many brain tangles and much joy.

Patrick Phillips was born and raised in Marin County, California. He plans to be successful enough to require only one name—Patty—like Moses or Cher.

Rebecca Shepard is a junior at Sarah Lawrence College. She has published poetry, fiction, and nonfiction online and in various literary magazines.

Melvin Jules Bukiet has written eight books of fiction and edited three anthologies. Several years ago he was a student at Sarah Lawrence College, where he now teaches.